everclear

Songs From An American...
Vol. One: Learning How To...

Transcribed by Hemme Luttjeboer

Project Manager: Jeannette DeLisa
Music Editor: Colgan Bryan
Book Art Layout: Debbie Johns
Album Artwork ©2000 Capitol Records, Inc.
Cover Concept: A. P. Alexakis
Photos: Frank W. Ockenfels III

WARNER BROS. PUBLICATIONS - THE GLOBAL LEADER IN PRINT
USA: 15800 NW 48th Avenue, Miami, FL 33014

WARNER/CHAPPELL MUSIC
CANADA: 15800 N.W. 48th AVENUE
MIAMI, FLORIDA 33014
SCANDINAVIA: P.O. BOX 533, VENDEVAGEN 85 B
S-182 15, DANDERYD, SWEDEN
AUSTRALIA: P.O. BOX 353
3 TALAVERA ROAD, NORTH RYDE N.S.W. 2113
ASIA: UNIT 901 - LIPPO SUN PLAZA
28 CANTON ROAD
TSIM SHA TSUI, KOWLOON, HONG KONG

Carisch NUOVA CARISCH
ITALY: VIA CAMPANIA, 12
20098 S. GIULIANO MILANESE (MI)
ZONA INDUSTRIALE SESTO ULTERIANO
SPAIN: MAGALLANES, 25
28015 MADRID
FRANCE: CARISCH MUSICOM,
25, RUE D'HAUTEVILLE, 75010 PARIS

IMP INTERNATIONAL MUSIC PUBLICATIONS LIMITED
ENGLAND: GRIFFIN HOUSE,
161 HAMMERSMITH ROAD, LONDON W6 8BS
GERMANY: MARSTALLSTR. 8, D-80539 MUNCHEN
DENMARK: DANMUSIK, VOGNMAGERGADE 7
DK 1120 KOBENHAVNK

© 2000 WARNER BROS. PUBLICATIONS
All Rights Reserved

Any duplication, adaptation or arrangement of the compositions
contained in this collection requires the written consent of the Publisher.
No part of this book may be photocopied or reproduced in any way without permission.
Unauthorized uses are an infringement of the U.S. Copyright Act and are punishable by law.

contents

Song From An American
Movie pt. 1
Page 3

Learning How To Smile
Page 44

Otis Redding
Page 71

Here We Go Again
Page 8

The Honeymoon Song
Page 50

Unemployed Boyfriend
Page 77

AM Radio
Page 19

Now That It's Over
Page 59

Wonderful
Page 88

Brown Eyed Girl
Page 33

Thrift Store Chair
Page 65

Annabella's Song
Page 99

SONGS FROM AN AMERICAN MOVIE PT. 1

lyrics by alexakis
music by everclear

Moderately ♩ = 78

Intro:

N.C.
(G)

Mandolin *(arr. for gtr.)* left-channel
Rhy. Fig. 1   **end Rhy. Fig. 1**

mf hold throughout

Banjo *(arr. for gtr.)* right-channel

mf hold throughout

Acous. Gtr.1 *(dbld. by 12-string acous.)*

© 2000 evergleam music / montalupis music / commongreen music / irving music, inc. (BMI)
all rights reserved

G
21 34
Rhy. Fig. 1A
end Rhy. Fig. 1A
Rhy. Fig. 1B
end Rhy. Fig. 1B
hold throughout

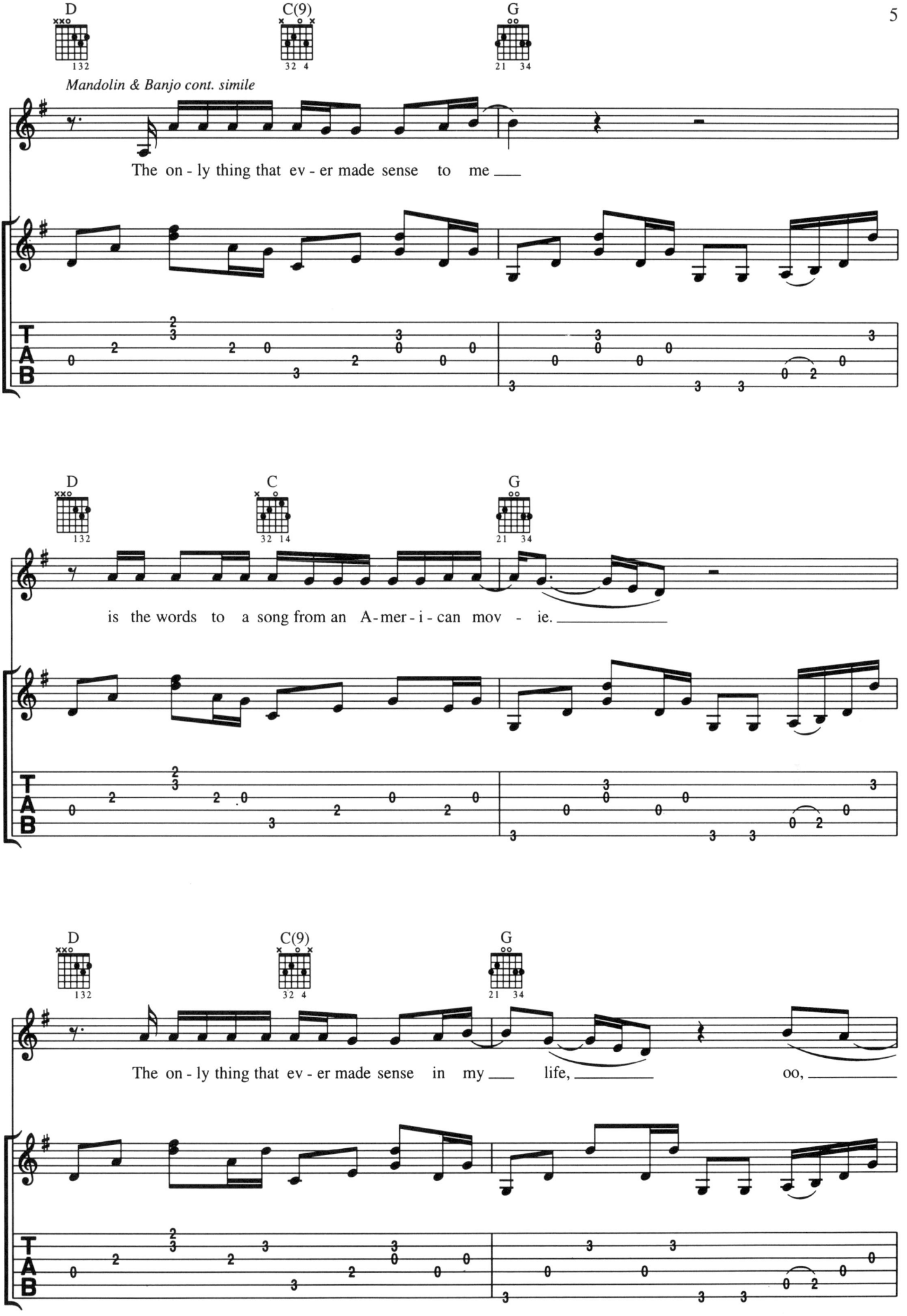

Verse:

The on-ly thing that ev-er made sense to me

is the words to a song from an A-mer-i-can mov-ie.

The on-ly thing that ev-er made sense in my life, oo,

is the sound of my lit-tle girl laugh-ing through the win-dow of a sum-mer night.

I sit a-lone in the back-yard wish-ing I could be in - side.

Just the sound of my lit-tle girl laugh-ing makes me hap-py just to be a-live.

Outro:
Chorus:
w/Rhy. Figs. 1 *(Mandolin)* **& 1A** *(Banjo) 7 times, simile*
w/Rhy. Fig. 1B *(Acous. Gtr. 1) 6 times, simile*

Makes me hap - py just to be a - live.

Bkgd. Vcl.: Oo,

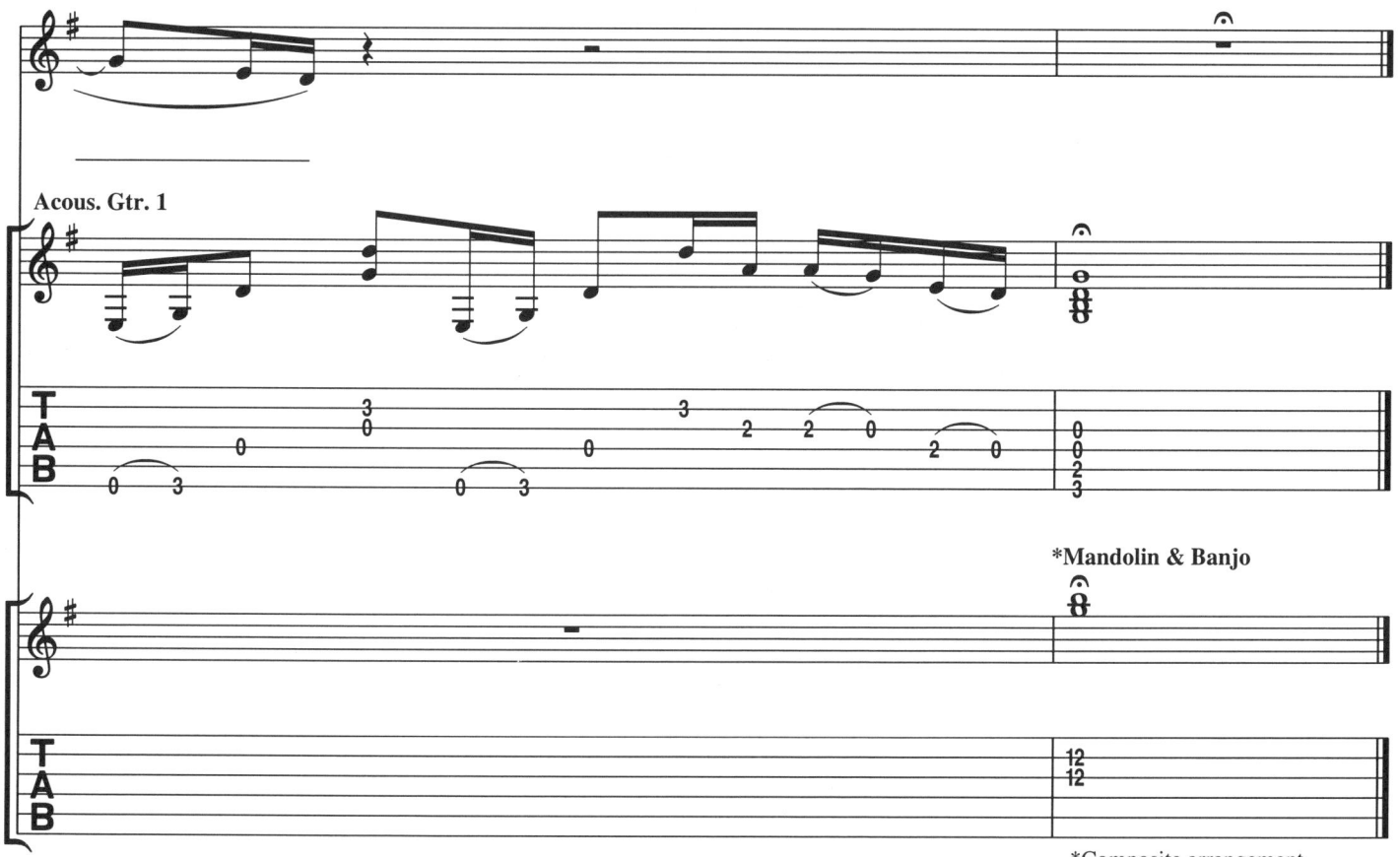

It makes me hap - py just to be a - live.

oo,

It makes me hap - py just to be a - live.

oo.

Acous. Gtr. 1

*Mandolin & Banjo

*Composite arrangement.

Songs From an American Movie Pt. 1 – 5 – 5
0467B

HERE WE GO AGAIN

lyrics by alexakis
music by everclear

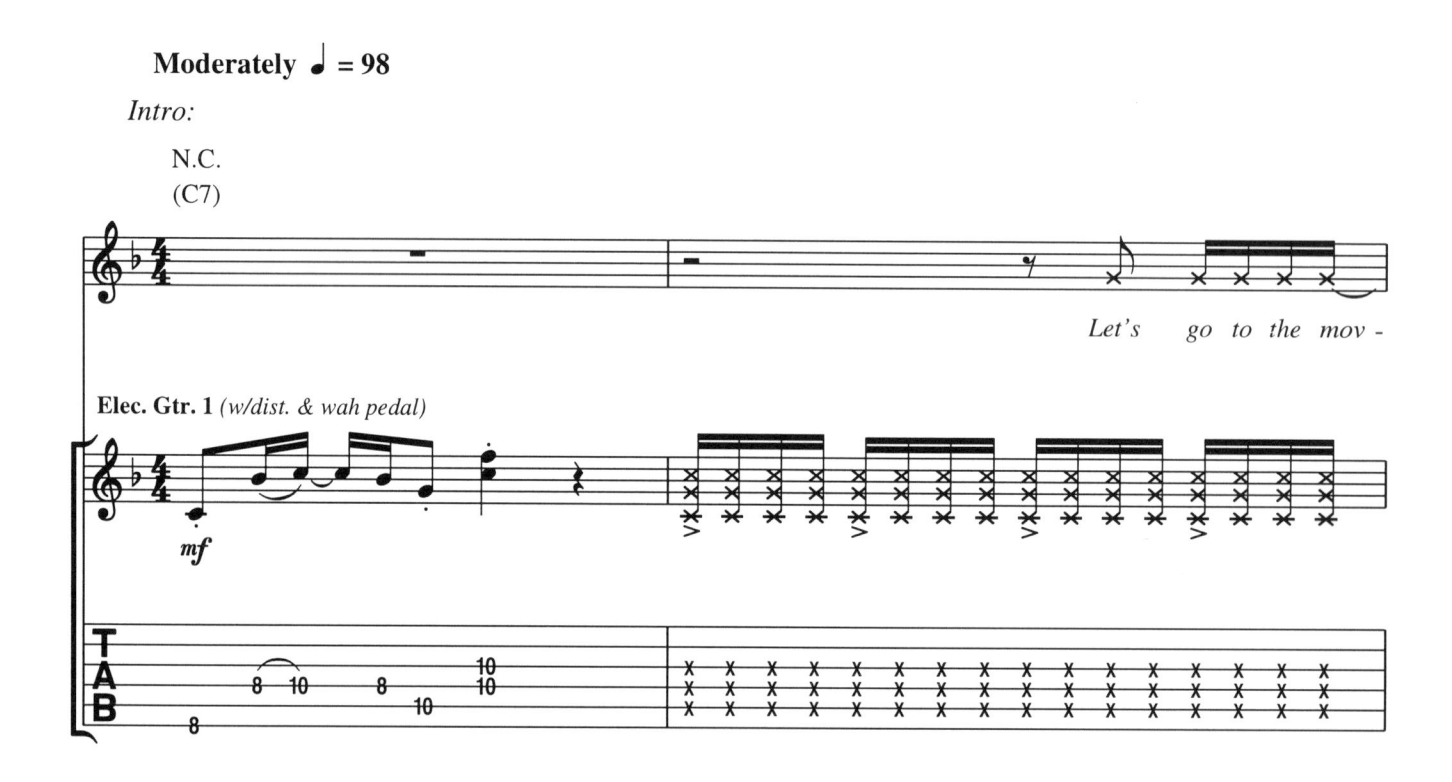

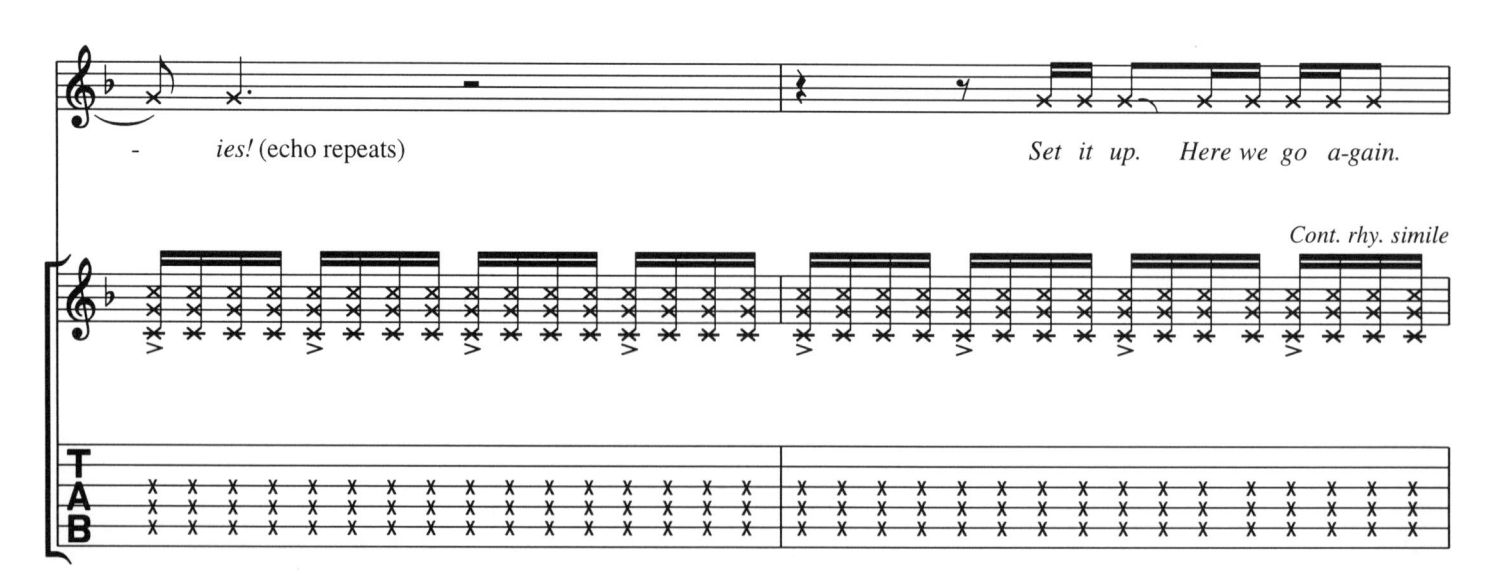

Moderately ♩ = 98

Intro:
N.C.
(C7)

Let's go to the mov-

Elec. Gtr. 1 *(w/dist. & wah pedal)*

-ies! (echo repeats)   *Set it up. Here we go a-gain.*

Cont. rhy. simile

Here We Go Again – 11 – 1
0467B

© 2000 evergleam music / montalupis music / commongreen music / irving music, inc. (BMI)
all rights reserved
"HERE WE GO AGAIN" contains a sample from "BRING THE NOISE" by Eric Sadler,
Carlton Ridenhour and James Henry Boxley
© 1987, 1988 Songs of Universal, Inc. and Bring the Noize, Inc.
All Rights Reserved

C7
3 2 4 (1)
C♯7
3 2 4 (1)
Set it up. Here we go a - gain.
Elec. Gtr. 2 (clean-tone, dbld.)
Rhy. Fig. 1
end Rhy. Fig. 1
mf
C7
C♯7
C9
2 1 3 3 3
1. Oo, ___
you know I like to watch you
Elec. Gtr. 3 (clean-tone)
-1/2
+1/2
w/bar

%: *Verse:*
w/Rhy. Fig. 1 *(Elec. Gtr. 2) 3 1/2 times, simile*

| C7 | | | C#7 |

sleep, (sleep, sleep, sleep.) No... I don't want to touch you, you'll get
slide, (slide, slide.) Yeah, yes, I like it when you do that
3. See additional lyrics

Elec. Gtr. 1 *(w/wah)*

mad at me. _____ No, _____ I don't want to think a-bout the
slow glide. _____ Now, please don't bad talk all those

bad times. _____ Aw... an-y-one could have a bad
good times. _____ Aw... don't ask for an-swers, ba-by,
(echo repeats)

Here We Go Again – 11 – 3
0467B

C7
324(1)
year. (echo repeats) Oo, now I don't want you to show
that you do not wan - na hear. Now, I don't want you to make
Elec. Gtr. 1
w/dist./wah off
Elec. Gtr. 2
Am
231
G
134211
F
134211
me. I do not want you to know me the way I used to be.
me. I do not need you to break me of all my child - ish ways.
Elec. Gtr. 1

All these good things we have would not mean a damn to me.
I'm still the same, you know, dumb, rock hard and good to go.

And I don't want to hear those words you feel you have to say when you
I still hear them voic - es call - ing me from back in the day.

find out how I used to be back in the day. 2. Yeah, you know I like the way you
Aw ba - by... can't you see there

ain't no place I'd rath-er be than watch-ing dirt-y mov-ies in that hap-py room with you. Sleep-ing on a mat-tress in the cor- ner, eat-ing Chi-nese food. I hear that voice in my head

1.
G
C9
C#9
Elec. Gtrs. 1 & 3 (on D.S.)
12fr
Elec. Gtr. 3
say, "Here we go a - gain."
Oo, now here we go a - gain.
C9
C#9
C9
D.S. 𝄋
Now, here we go a - gain.
Ah.
3. I know you like the way I
2.
w/Rhy. Fig. 1 (Elec. Gtr. 2)
C9
C#9
C9
Elec. Gtr. 3
(echo repeats)
Yeah, here we go a - gain.
Aw,

C♯9
C9
21333
ba - by... here we go a - gain.
I know, I know, I know, I know, I
Elec. Gtr. 1
know, I know, I know, I know, Aw ba - by, ba - by, can't you see?
Bkgd. Vcl.: know, I know, I know, I know.
8va
F
G
134211
Yes, I know you got some doubts, I know you don't be - lieve. I

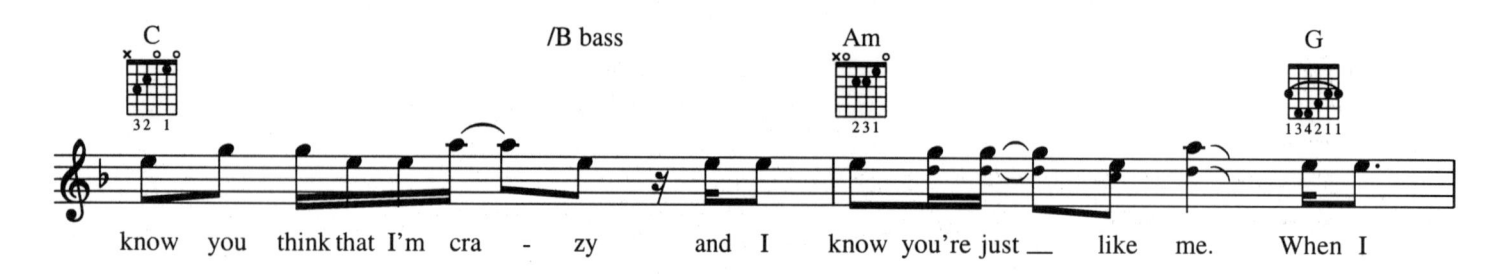

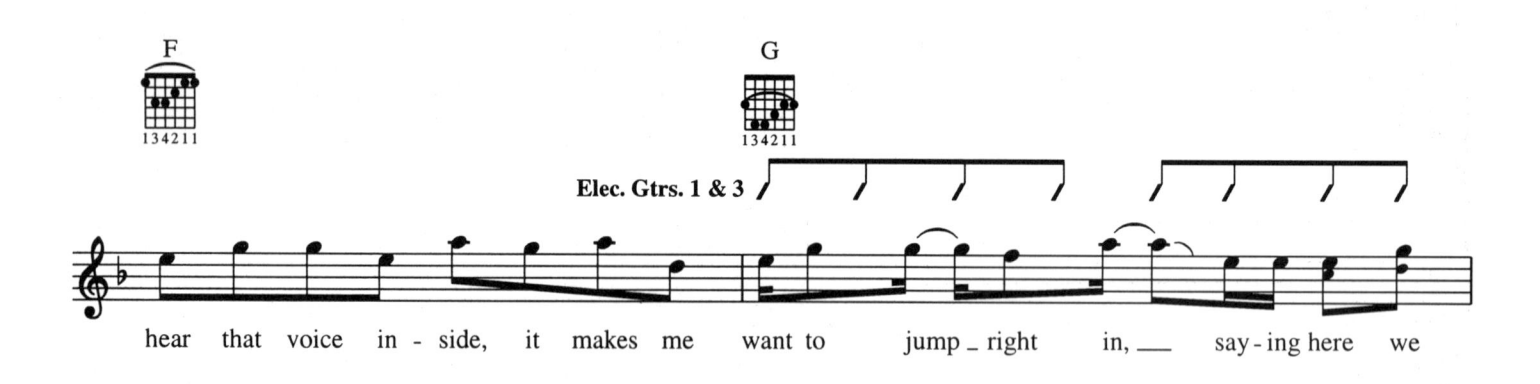

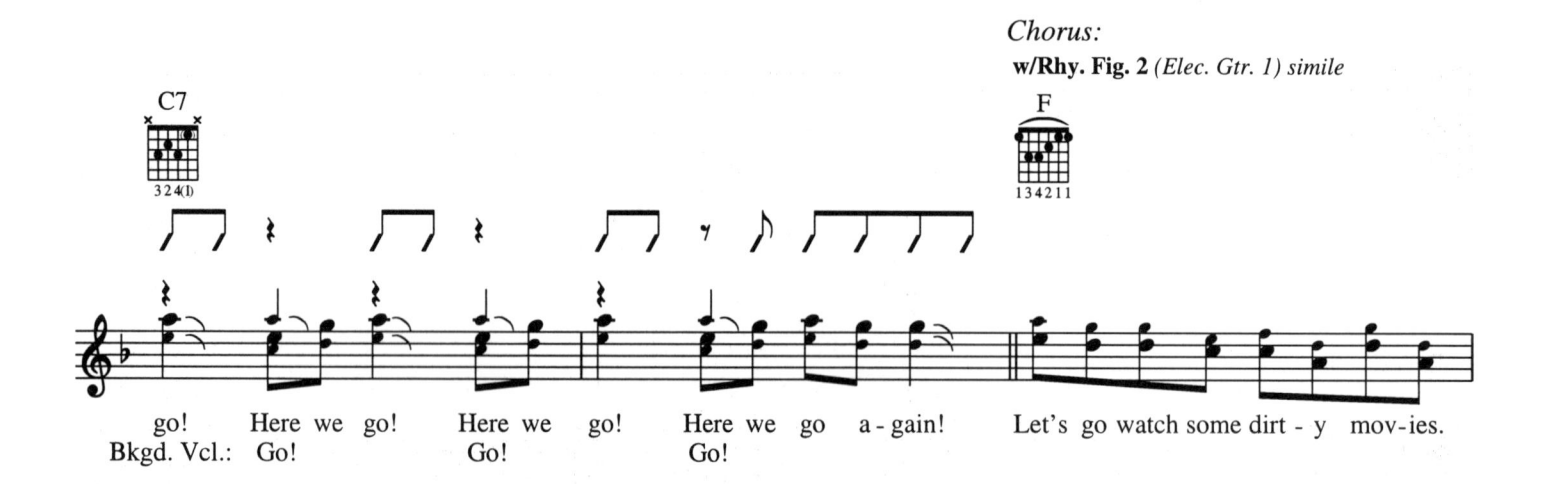

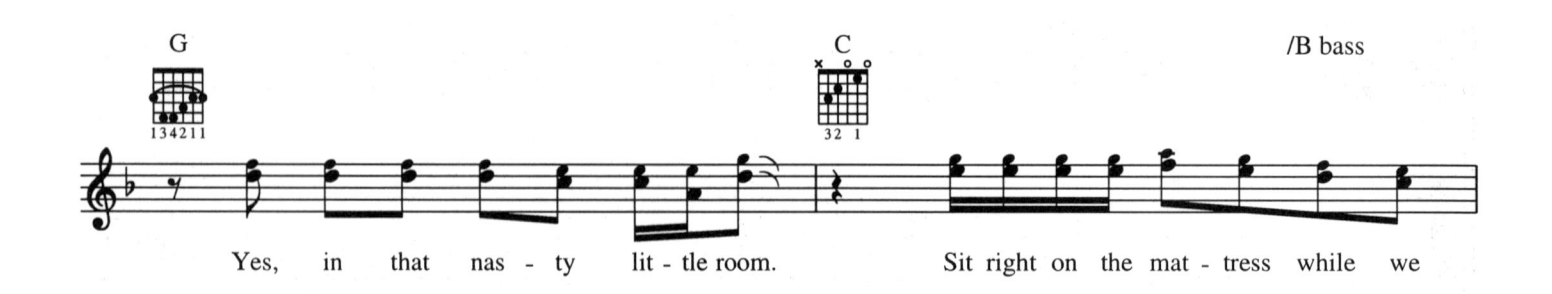

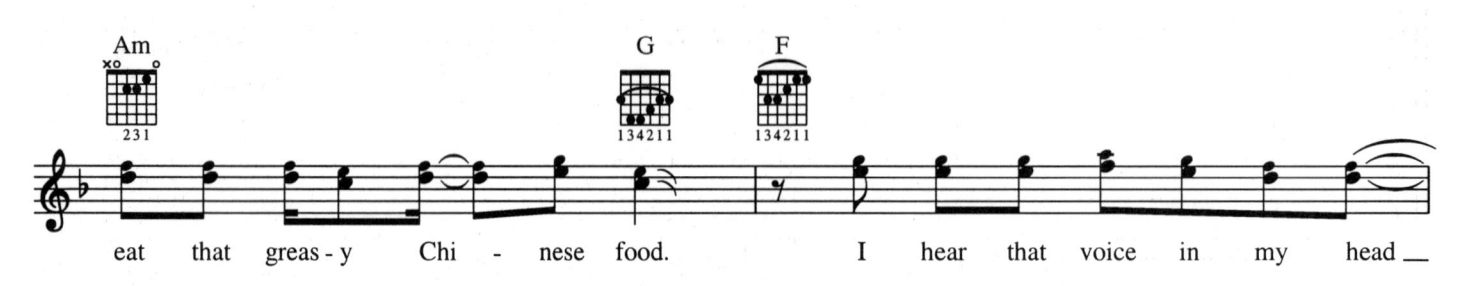

[C] know you think that I'm cra-zy [/B bass] and I [Am] know you're just __ like me. [G] When I

[F] hear that voice in-side, it makes me want to [G] jump right in, __ say-ing here we

Chorus:
w/Rhy. Fig. 2 *(Elec. Gtr. 1) simile*

[C7] go! Here we go! Here we go! Here we go a-gain! [F] Let's go watch some dirt-y mov-ies.
Bkgd. Vcl.: Go! Go! Go!

[G] Yes, in that nas-ty lit-tle room. [C] Sit right on the mat-tress while we [/B bass]

[Am] eat that greas-y Chi-nese food. [G] [F] I hear that voice in my head __

G
134211
C7
324(1)
say, "Here we go a - gain."
Elec. Gtr. 3
Elec. Gtr. 2
Elec. Gtr. 1
C#9
21333
C9
21333
Elec. Gtr. 3
Oooh...
w/flanger
1/2

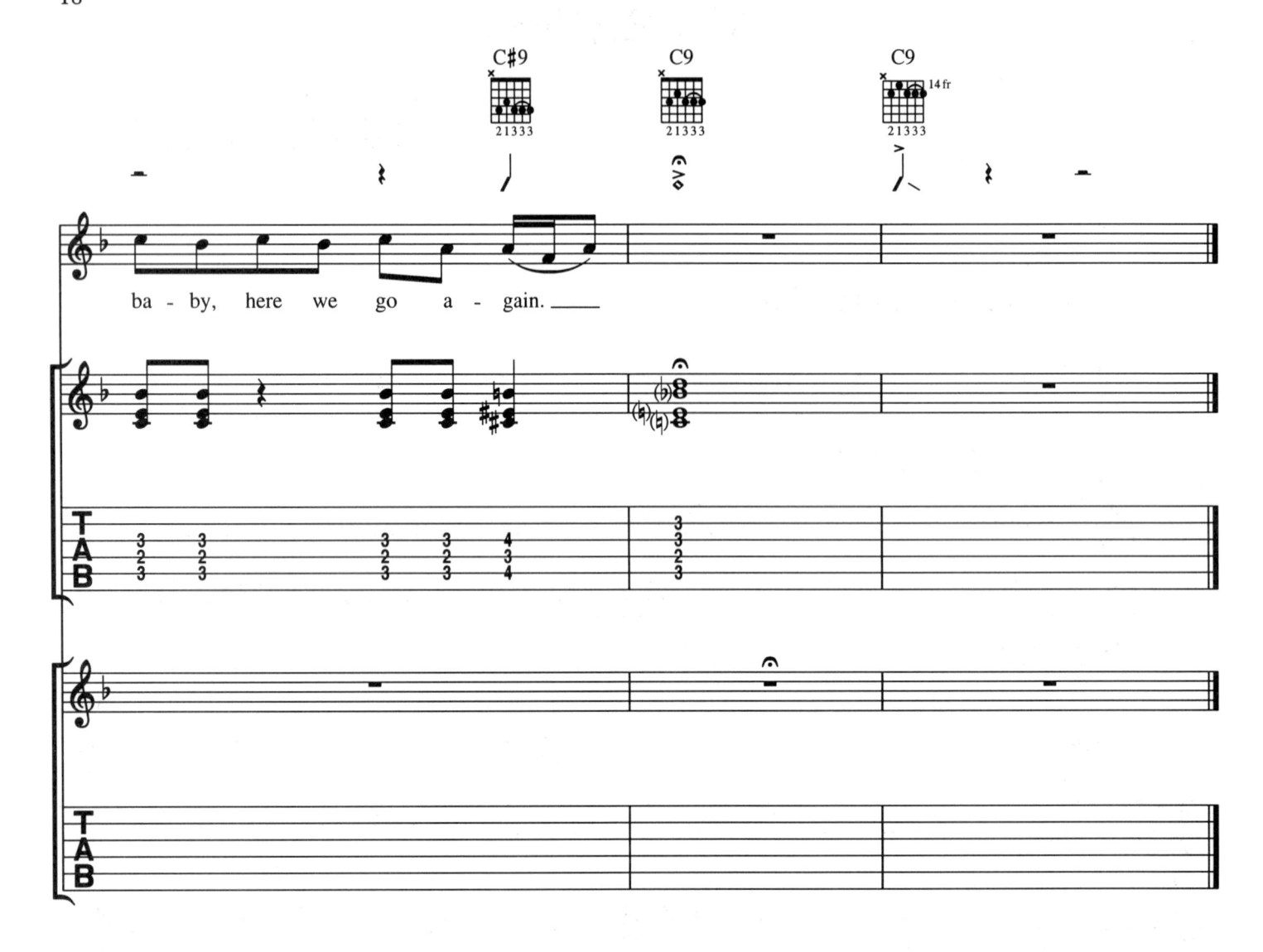

Verse 3:
I know you like the way I rock.
Sometimes I just need to drown
Out all that back talk.
I could not care less what your friends say.
Someone's always talking s*** about the old days.

You do not need to remind me
That I left it all behind
Those things I used to do.
I don't want that other life 'cause
I am so in love with you.
I can barely hear it calling me
From back in the day.

Aw baby... can't you see
There ain't no place I'd rather be...
(To Chorus:)

AM RADIO

lyrics by alexakis
music by everclear, carol washington,
ralph williams and joseph broussard

All Gtrs. tune down 1/2 step:
- ⑥ = E♭   ③ = G♭
- ⑤ = A♭   ② = B♭
- ④ = D♭   ① = E♭

Moderately ♩ = 92

Intro:

DJ voices: *KHJ Los Angeles. Portions of today's programming are reproduced by means of electrical transcriptions or tape recordings.*

Elec. Gtr. 1 *(clean-tone)*
mf

Bkgd. Oo,   oo.   Ah.
Vcl.:   oo.

AM Radio – 14 – 1
0467B

© 2000 evergleam music / montalupis music / commongreen music / irving music, inc. (BMI) / malaco music / caraljo music
all rights reserved
"AM RADIO" contains samples from "MR. BIG STUFF" by Carol Washington, Ralph Williams and Joseph Broussard
© Malaco Music and Caraljo Music and "THOSE WERE THE DAYS" by Charles Strouse and Lee Adams © EMI Worldtrax Music Inc.
All Rights Reserved

Verse 1:

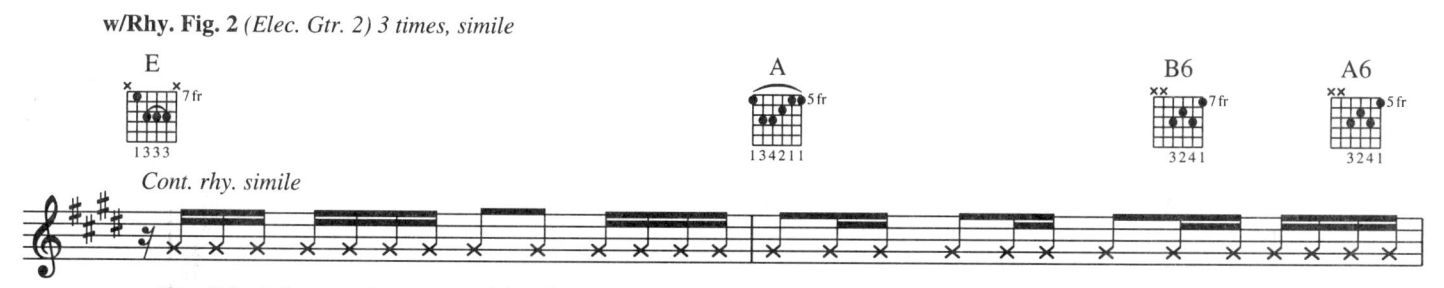

The V C R and the D V D, there was-n't none of that crap back in nine-teen sev-en-ty.

We did-n't know a-bout a world wide web. It was a whole dif-f'rent game be-ing played back when I was a kid.

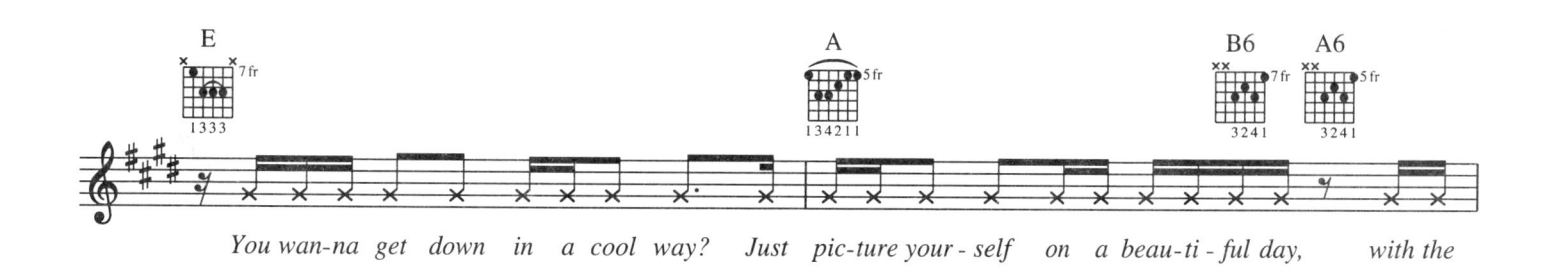

You wan-na get down in a cool way? Just pic-ture your-self on a beau-ti-ful day, with the

big bell bot-toms and groov-y long hair, just a walk-ing in style with a por-ta-ble C D play-

22

Chorus:
w/Rhy. Figs. 1 *(Elec. Gtr. 3)* **& 1A** *(Elec. Gtr. 2) 2 times, simile*

-er. No... no, you would lis-ten to the mu-sic on the A M ra-di-o, (A M ra-di-o.)
Bkgd. Vcl. Oo! (echo repeat)

Yeah... you could hear the mu-sic A M ra-di-o, A M ra-di-o, A M ra-di-o. ___ Oo!

Verse 2:
w/Rhy. Fig. 2 *(Elec. Gtr. 2) 4 times, simile*

Flash back (back) to sev-en-ty-two, __ an-oth-er sum-mer in the neigh-bor-hood, hang-ing out with noth-ing to do. __

Cont. rhy. simile

___ Some-times we'd go driv-ing a-round __ in my sis-ter's Pin-to, cruis-in' with the win-dows rolled

Bkgd. Vcl. Fig. 2 ... **end Bkgd. Vcl. Fig. 2**

down. We'd lis-ten to the ra-di-o sta-tion, we were too damn poor to buy the eight-track tapes. There
Bkgd. Vcl.: Oo, oo, oo, oo.

AM Radio – 14 – 4
0467B

was-n't an - y good time to want to be in - side. My mom would want to watch that T V all god damn
Oo, oo, oo.

Bridge:

night. I'd be in bed with the ra - di - o on. ____ I would lis - ten to it all night

long, ____ just to hear my fa - vor - ite song. ____ *You'd have to wait but you could hear it on the*

Chorus:
w/Bkgd. Vcl. Fig. 1, 4 times, simile
w/Rhy. Figs. 1 (Elec. Gtr. 3) & 1A (Elec. Gtr. 2) 2 times, simile
E E9sus A A7 B7
A M ra - di - o. (echo repeats) Yeah, you could hear the mu - sic on the
E E9sus A A7 B7
A M ra - di - o. I can still hear ma - ma say, "Boy... turn that ra - di - o
Interlude:
E A B6 A6
Elec. Gtr. 1
down!!!!" Aw, mom, not that show a - gain. I don't wan-na watch that show,
Keybd. (arr. for gtr.) dbld. by Elec. Gtr. 4 (w/dist.)
mf
E A B6 A6
can't we watch "Good Times" or "Chi-co and the Man" or some-thin' cool? Turn it
hold

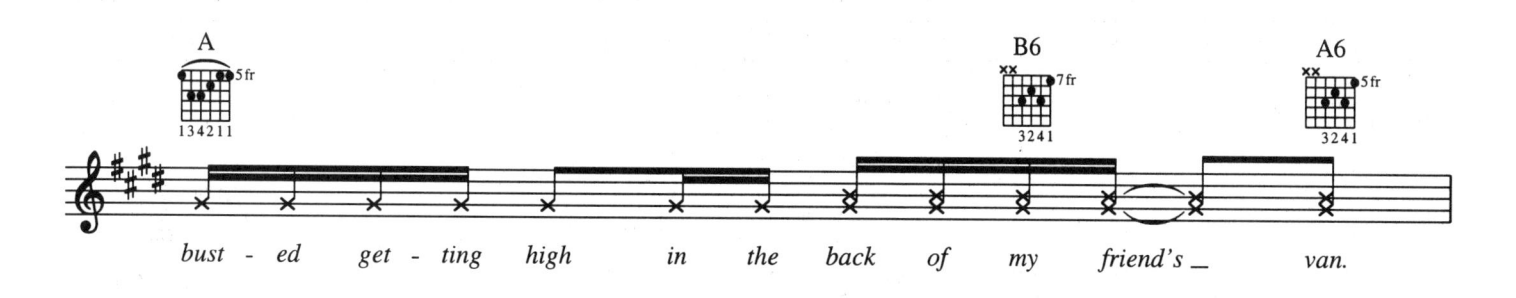

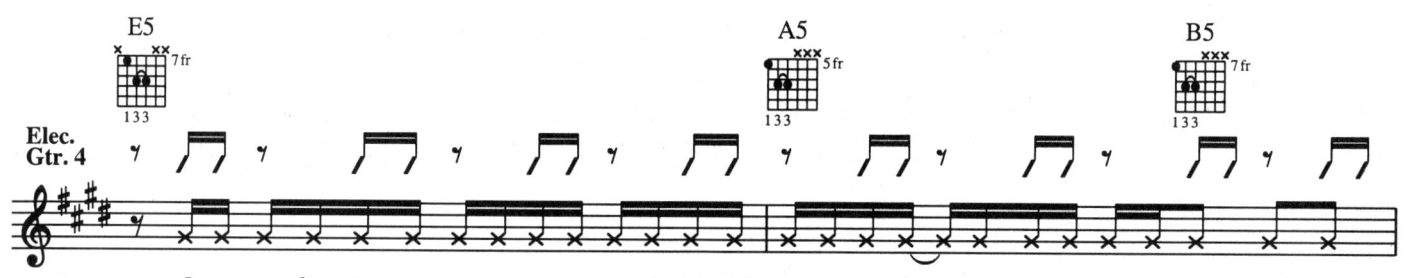

Verse 3:
w/Bkgd. Vcl. Fig. 2, *4 times, simile*
w/Rhy. Figs. 2 *(Elec. Gtr. 1)* **& 2A** *(Elec. Gtr. 2) 4 times, simile*

off, (turn it off, turn it off, turn it off.) ...Things changed back in sev-en-ty-five, __ we were
(echo repeats)

all grow-ing up on the in and the out - side. We got in trou-ble with the po - lice-man, we got

bust-ed get-ting high in the back of my friend's __ van.

I re-mem-ber nine-teen sev-en-ty-sev-en, I start-ed go-ing to con-certs and I saw the Led Zeppe-lin.

26

I got a guitar on Christmas day, I dreamed that Jimmy Page would come to Santa Monica and teach me to play!

Elec. Gtr. 5 (w/dist. & talkbox)

Bridge:
w/Rhy. Figs. 3 (Elec. Gtr. 4) & 3A (Elec. Gtr. 3) 1st 3 bars, simile

Play! Teach me to play, teach me to play, teach me to play,

teach me to play. Play, play, play, play, play.

AM Radio – 14 – 8
0467B

w/Rhy. Figs. 3 *(Elec. Gtr. 4)* & 3A *(Elec. Gtr. 3) simile*

There isn't any other place that I need to go. There isn't anything that I need to know

that I did not learn from the radio.

Interlude:

Yeah, when things get stu-pid and I just don't know where to

Chorus:

find my hap-py... I lis-ten to the mu-sic from the A M ra-di-o, (A M ra-di-o.)

You could hear the mu-sic on the A M ra-di-o, (A M ra-di-o.)

AM Radio – 14 – 10
0467B

Lyrics:

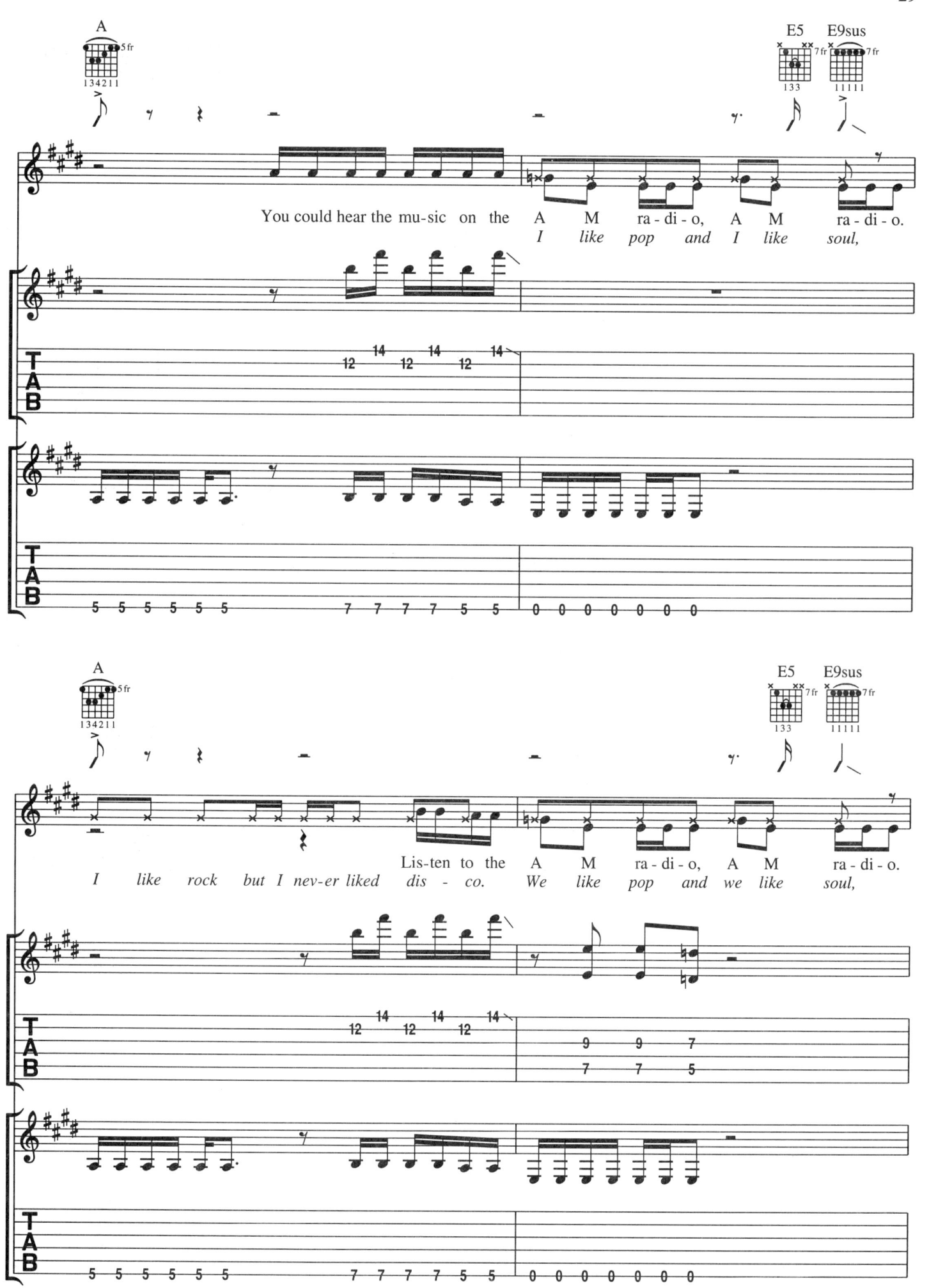

You could hear the music on the AM radio, AM radio.
I like pop and I like soul,
I like rock but I never liked disco.
Listen to the AM radio, AM radio.
We like pop and we like soul,

30

We like to rock but we never liked disco. AM radio, AM radio. We like pop and we like soul, we like to rock but we never liked disco.

AM Radio – 14 – 12
0467B

31

w/Rhy. Figs. 1 (Elec. Gtr. 3) & 1A (Elec. Gtr. 2) 2 times, simile

A M ra - di - o. A M ra - di - o.
We like rock 'n' roll, we like soul, we like to rock but we nev-er liked dis - co.

A M ra - di - o. A M ra - di - o.
We like rock 'n' roll, we like soul, we like to rock but we nev-er liked dis - co.

Outro Chorus:
w/Rhy. Figs. 1 (Elec. Gtr. 3) & 1A (Elec. Gtr. 2) 4 times, simile

A M ra - di - o, _____ A M ra - di - o,
Bkgd. Vcl.: No, I nev-er liked dis - co, no, I nev-er liked dis - co.

Elec. Gtr. 5

A M ra - di - o, _____ A M ra - di - o,
No, I nev-er liked dis - co, no, I nev-er liked dis - co. _____

w/talk box effect

AM Radio – 14 – 13
0467B

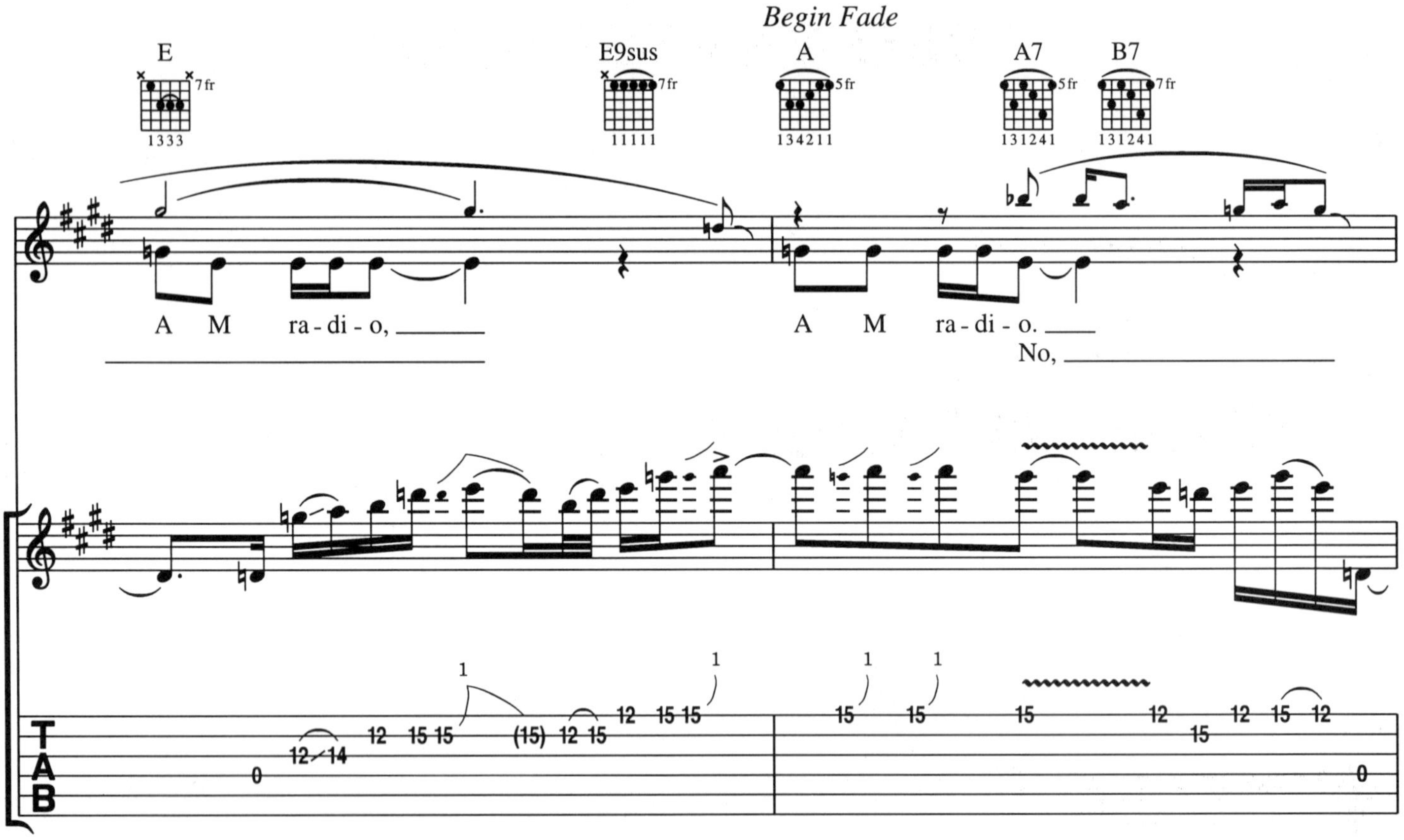
Begin Fade
E
E9sus
A
A7
B7
A M ra - di - o,
A M ra - di - o.
No,

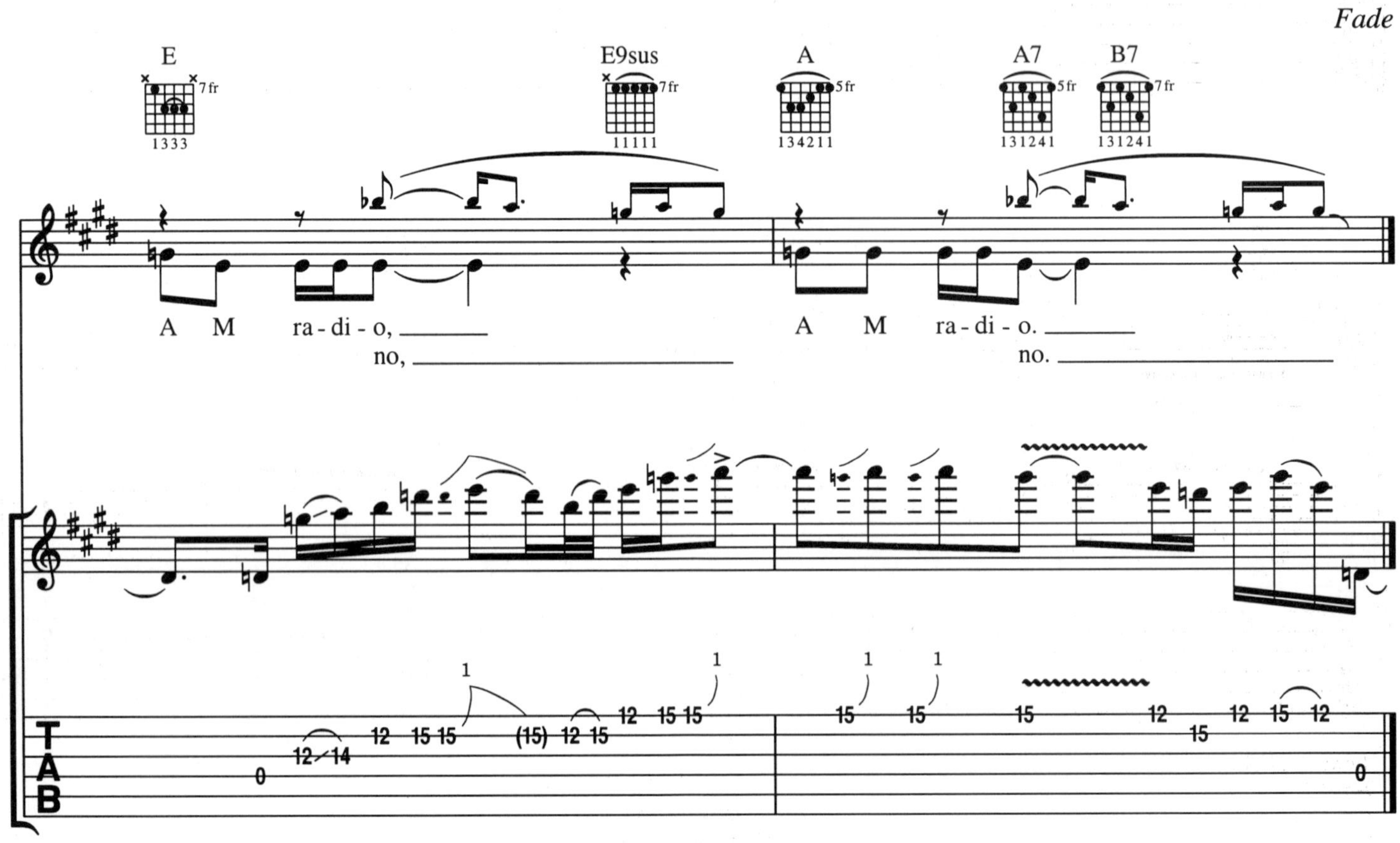
Fade
E
E9sus
A
A7
B7
A M ra - di - o,
no,
A M ra - di - o.
no.

BROWN EYED GIRL

words and music by
van morrison

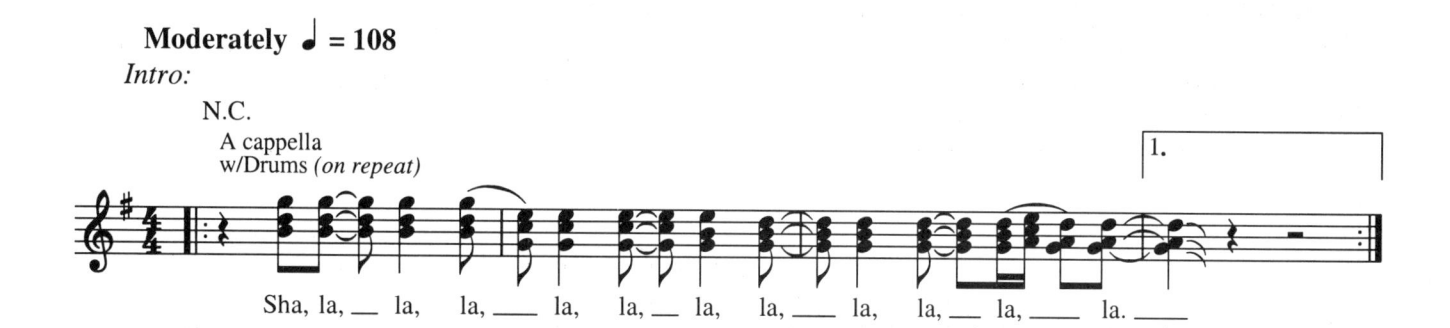

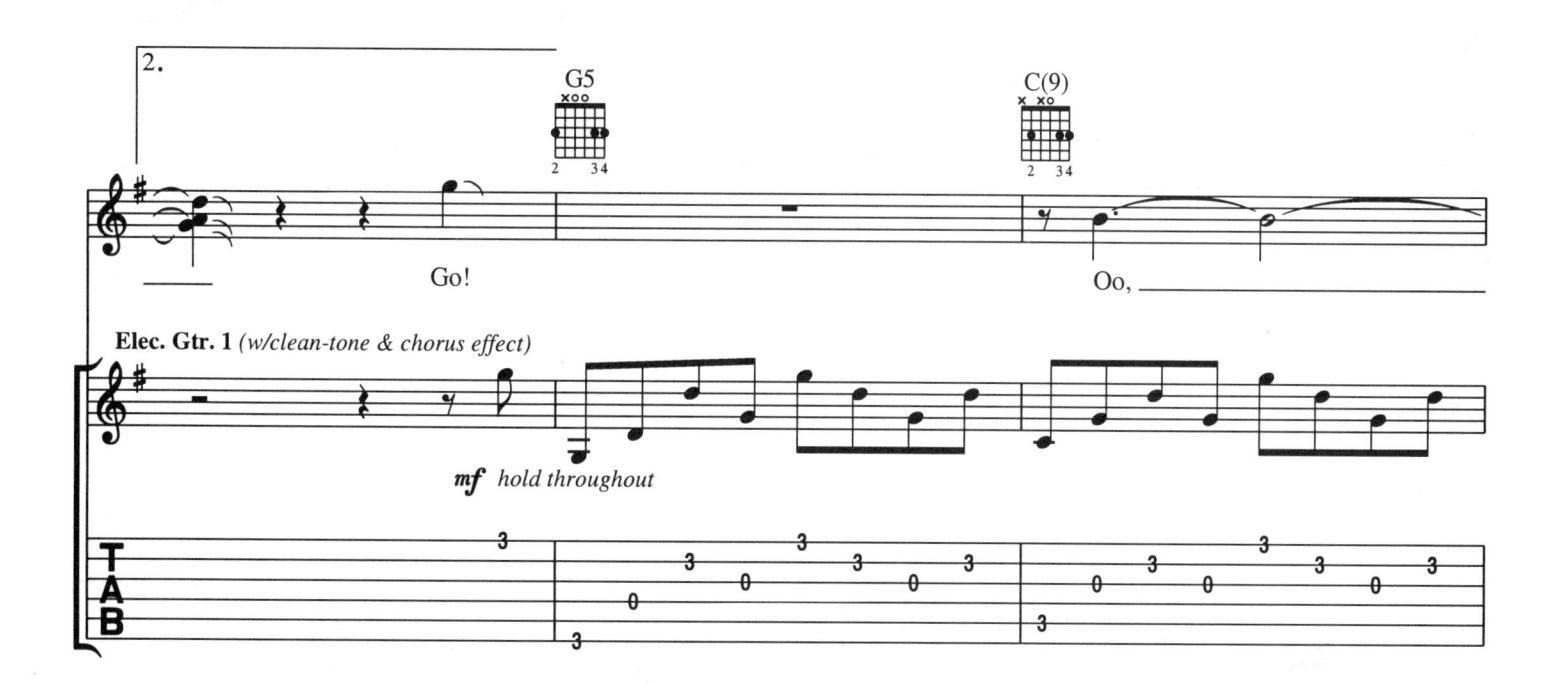

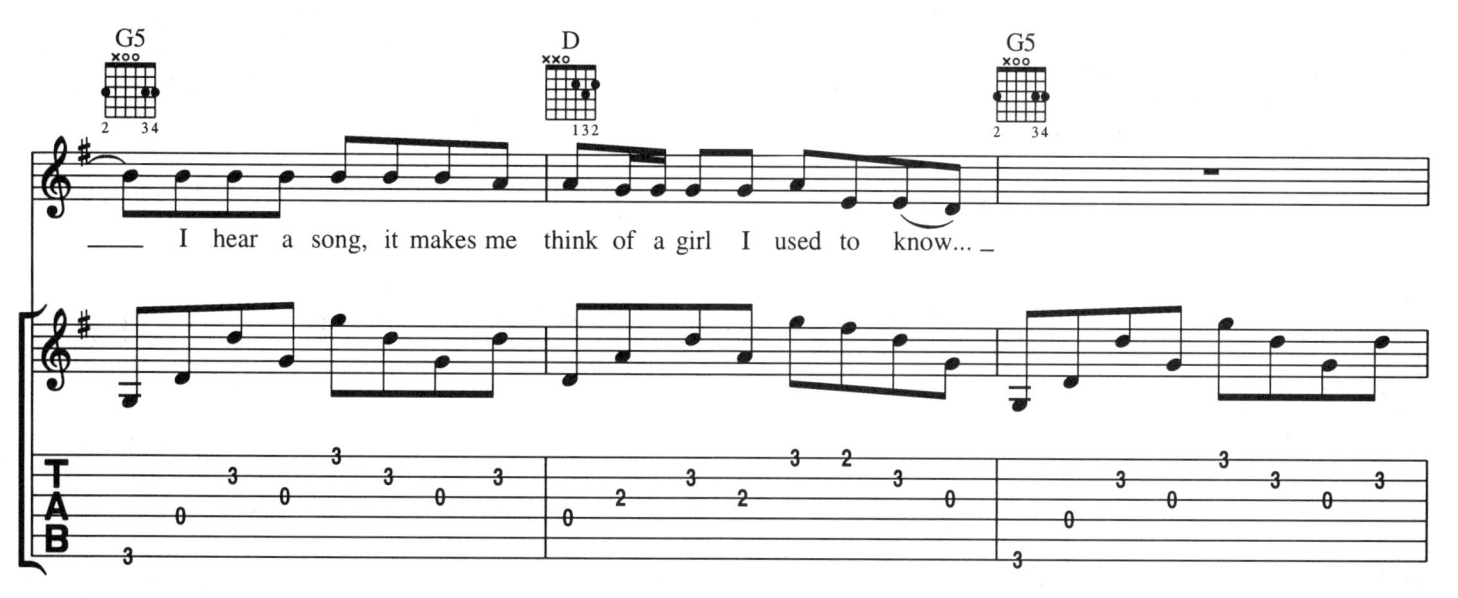

Moderately ♩ = 108

Intro:

N.C.
A cappella
w/Drums (on repeat)

Sha, la, la, la, la, la, la, la, la, la, la.

Go! Oo,

Elec. Gtr. 1 *(w/clean-tone & chorus effect)*

mf hold throughout

I hear a song, it makes me think of a girl I used to know...

Brown Eyed Girl – 11 – 1
0467B

© 1967 Web IV Music
Copyright Renewed
All Rights for the U.S. and Canada Controlled and Administered by Universal - Songs of PolyGram International, Inc.
All Rights Reserved

34

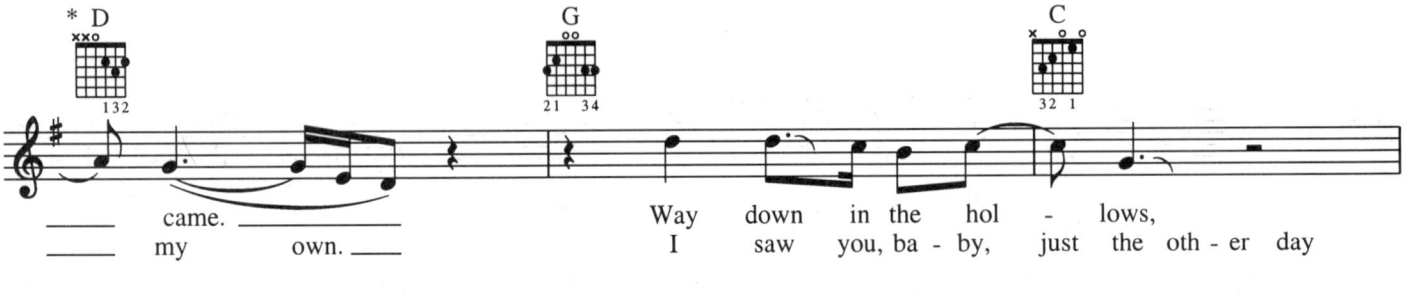

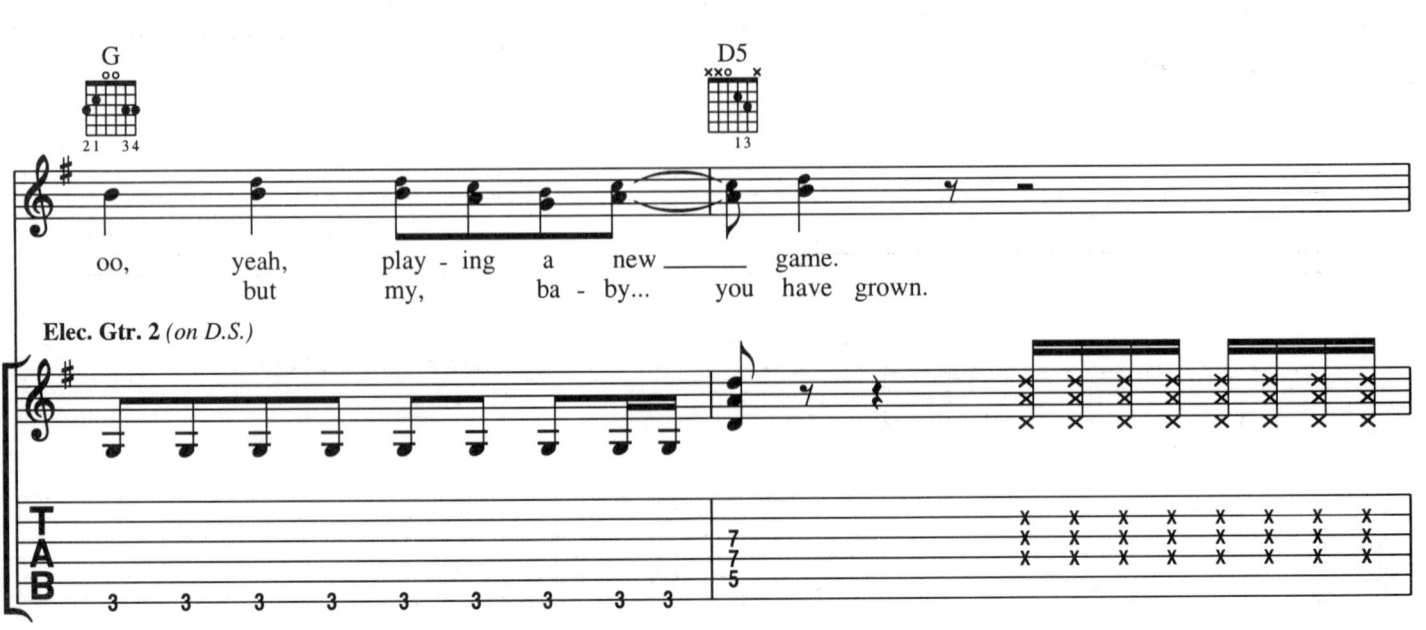

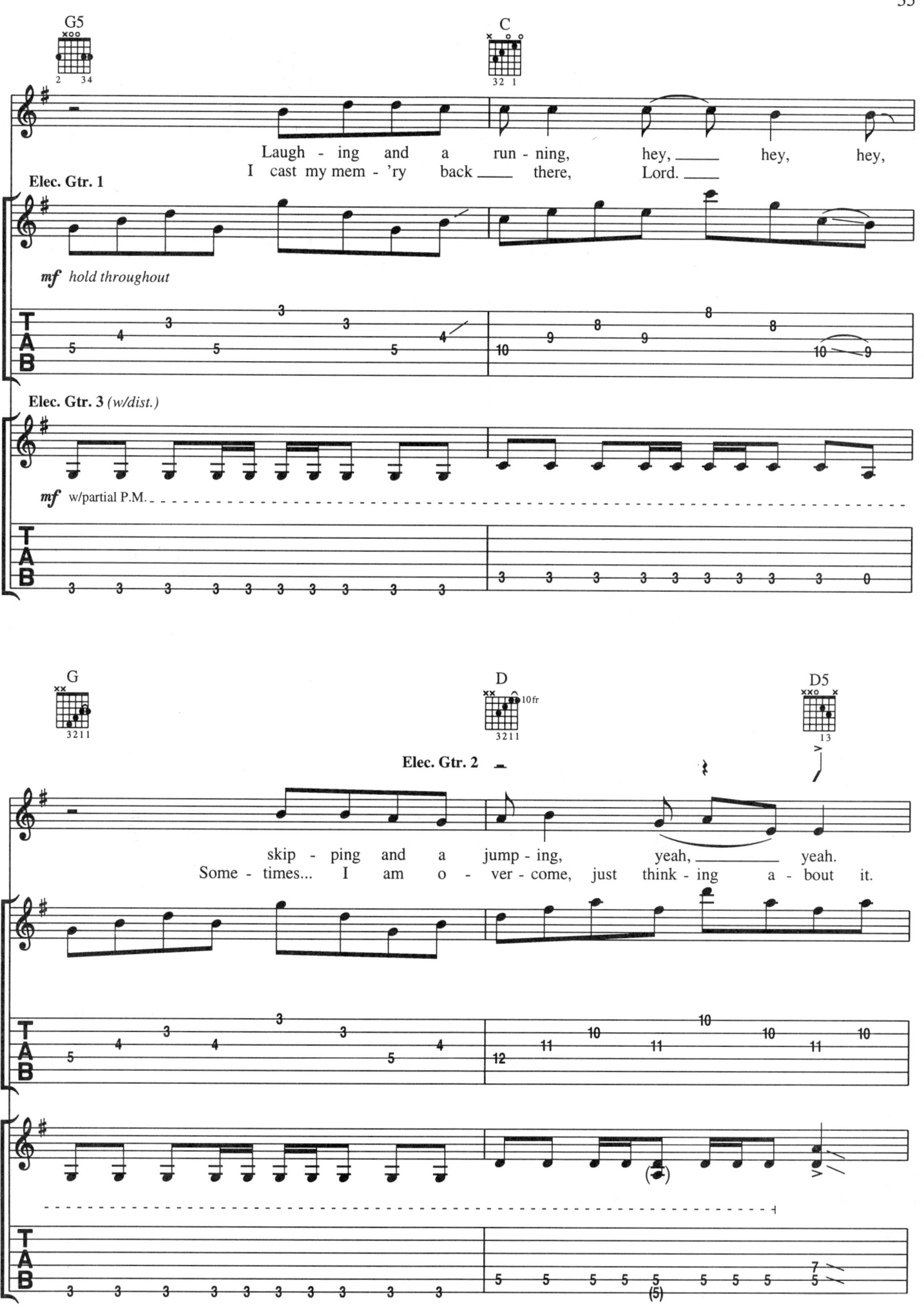

Laughing and a running, hey, hey, hey,
skipping and a jumping, yeah, yeah.

I cast my mem-'ry back there, Lord.
Sometimes... I am o-ver-come, just thinking about it.

Brown Eyed Girl – 11 – 3
0467B

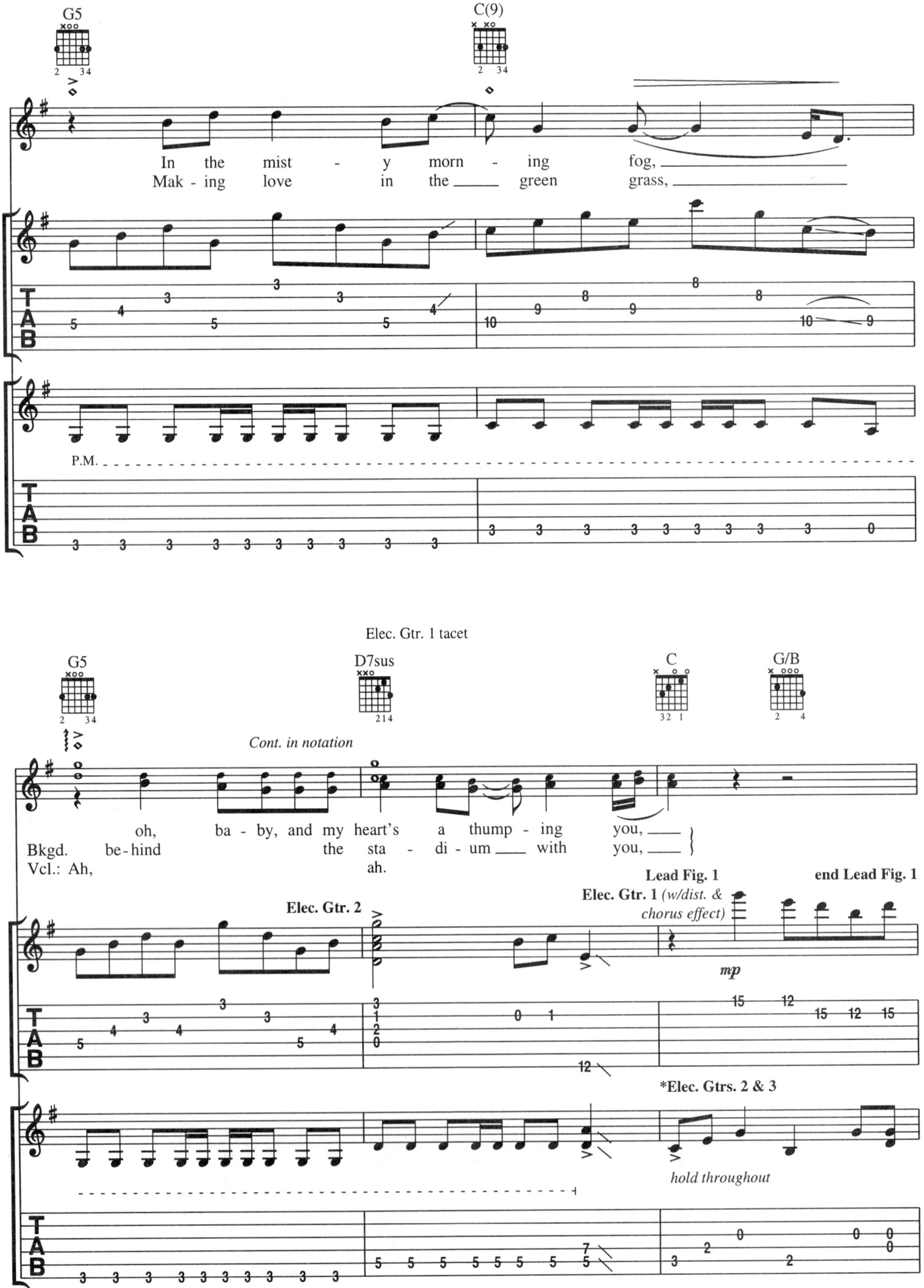

*Composite arrangement.

37

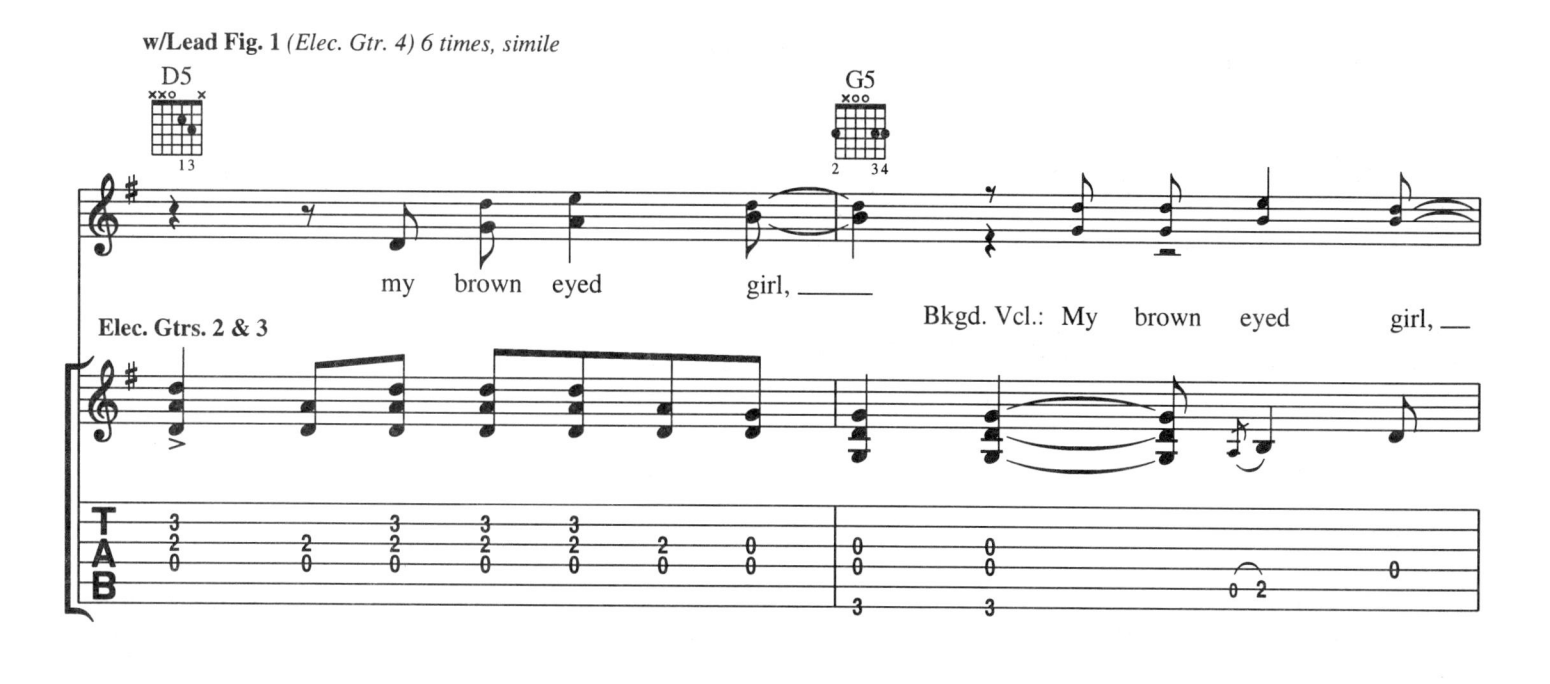

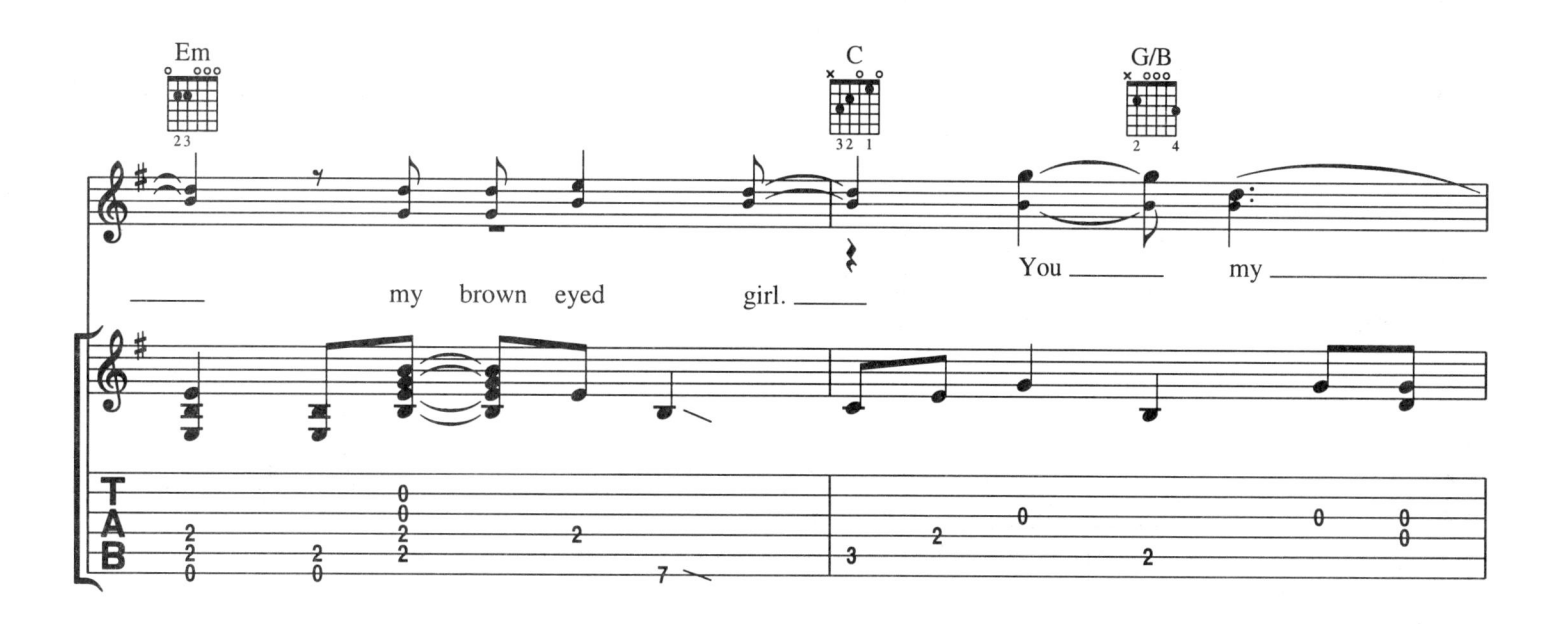

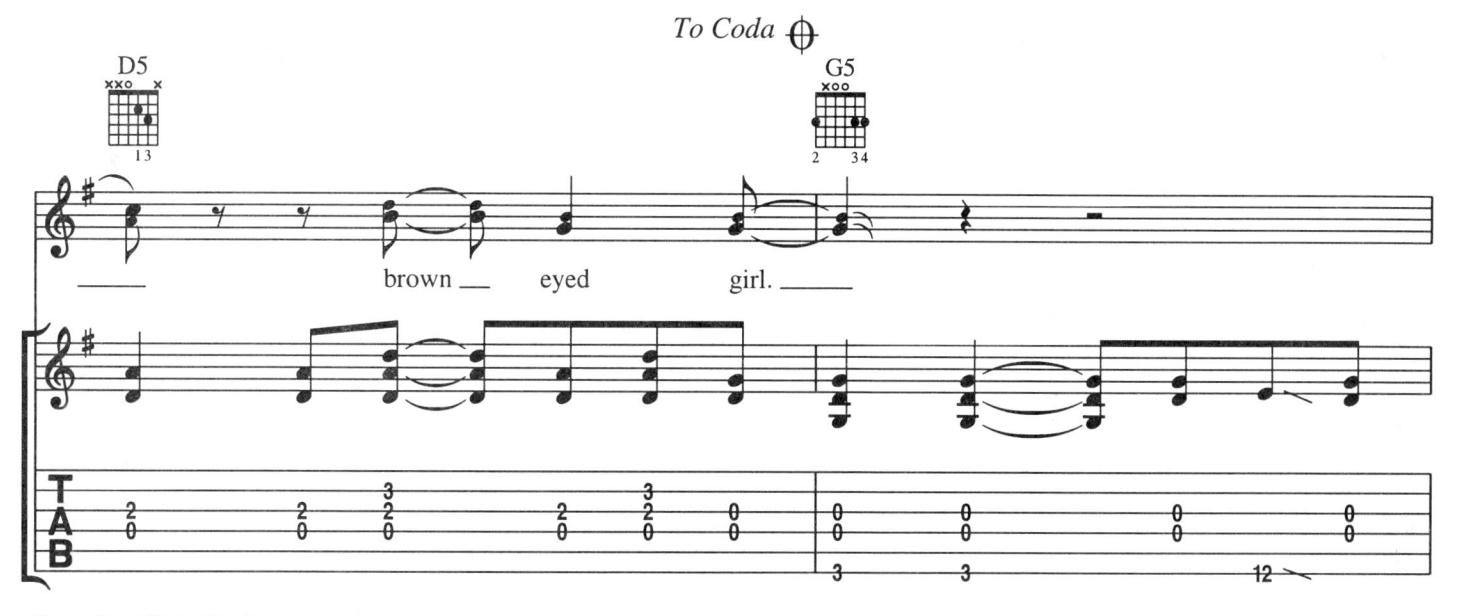

D
Do you re-mem-ber when? Yeah, we used to sing...
Do you re-mem-ber when?
Elec. Gtr. 1
hold throughout
Elec. Gtrs. 2 & 3
Chorus:
w/Lead Fig. 1 (Elec. Gtr. 4) 6 times, simile
G5
C(9)
Rhy. Fig. 1
*Elec. Gtrs. 1, 2, & 3
Sha, la, la, la, la, la, la, la,
*Composite arrangement.
G5
1.
D5
end Rhy. Fig. 1
2.
D5
la, la, la, la.
La, la.

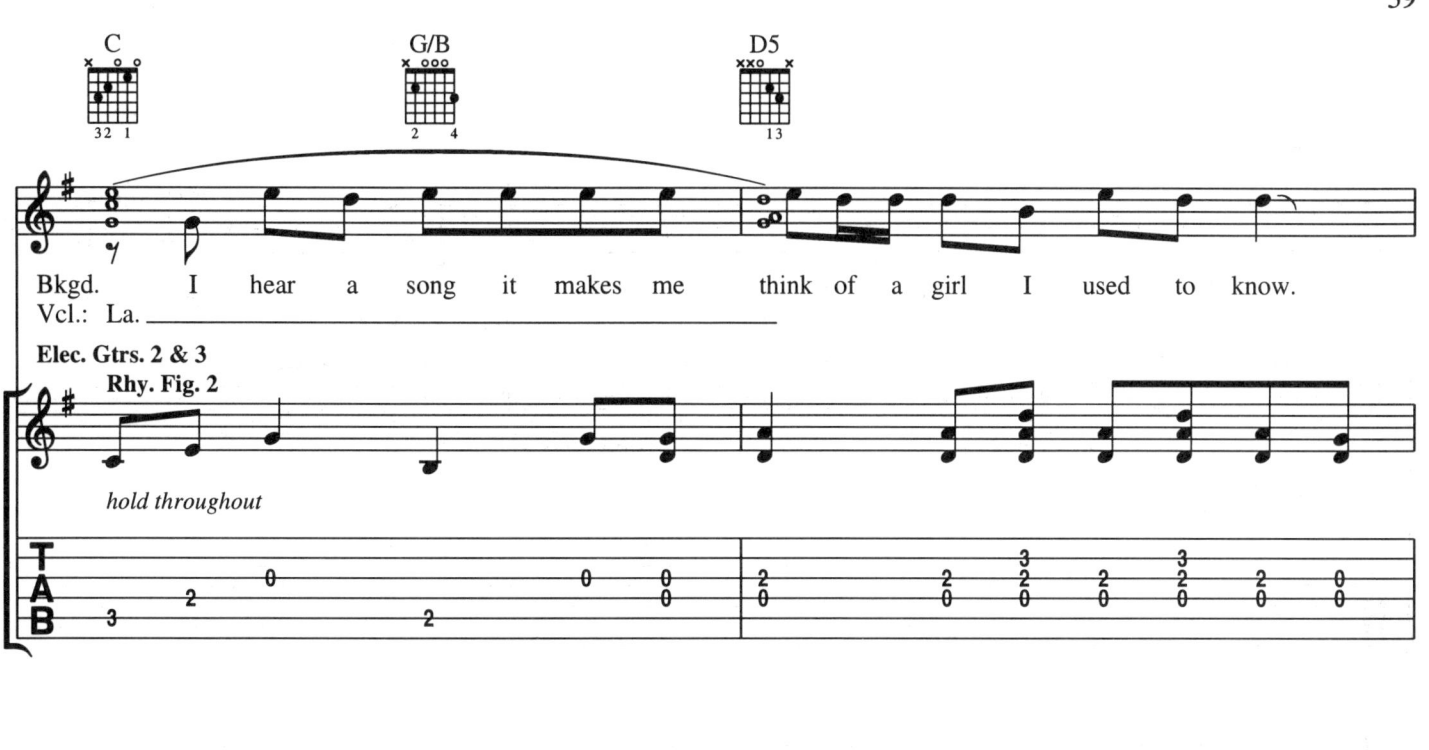

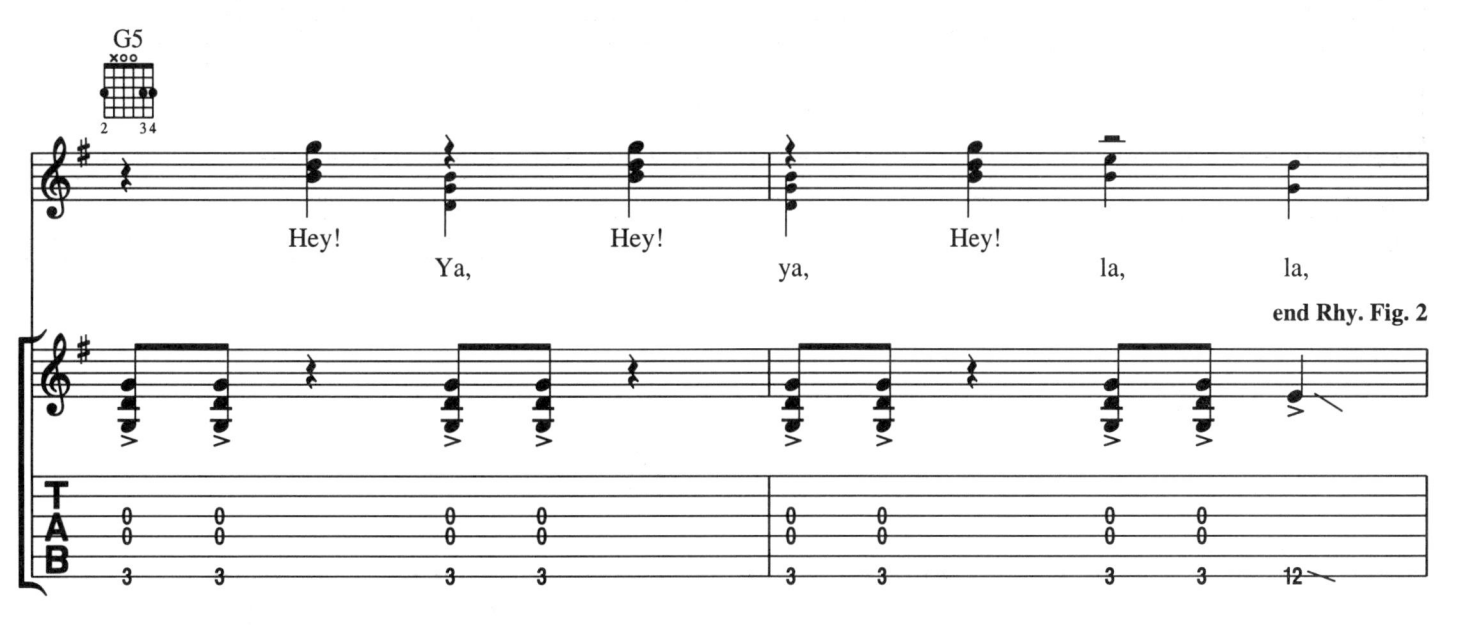

Brown Eyed Girl – 11 – 7
0467B

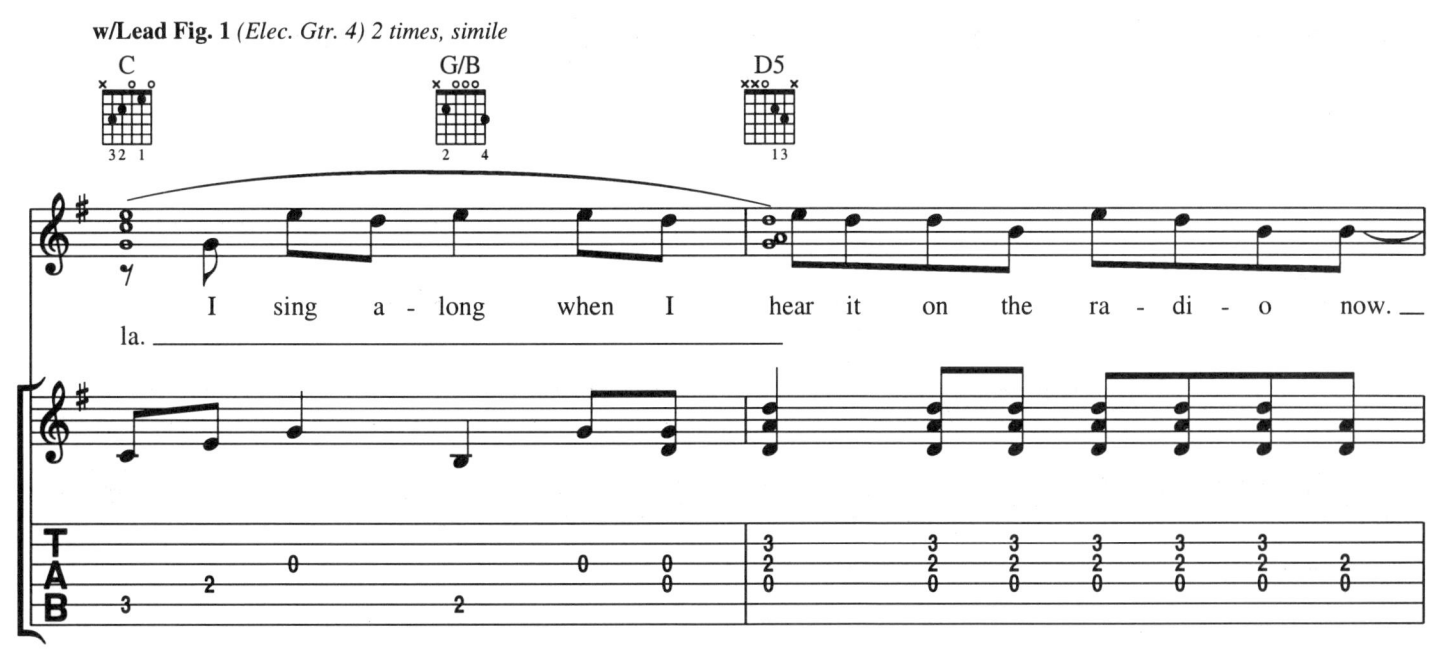

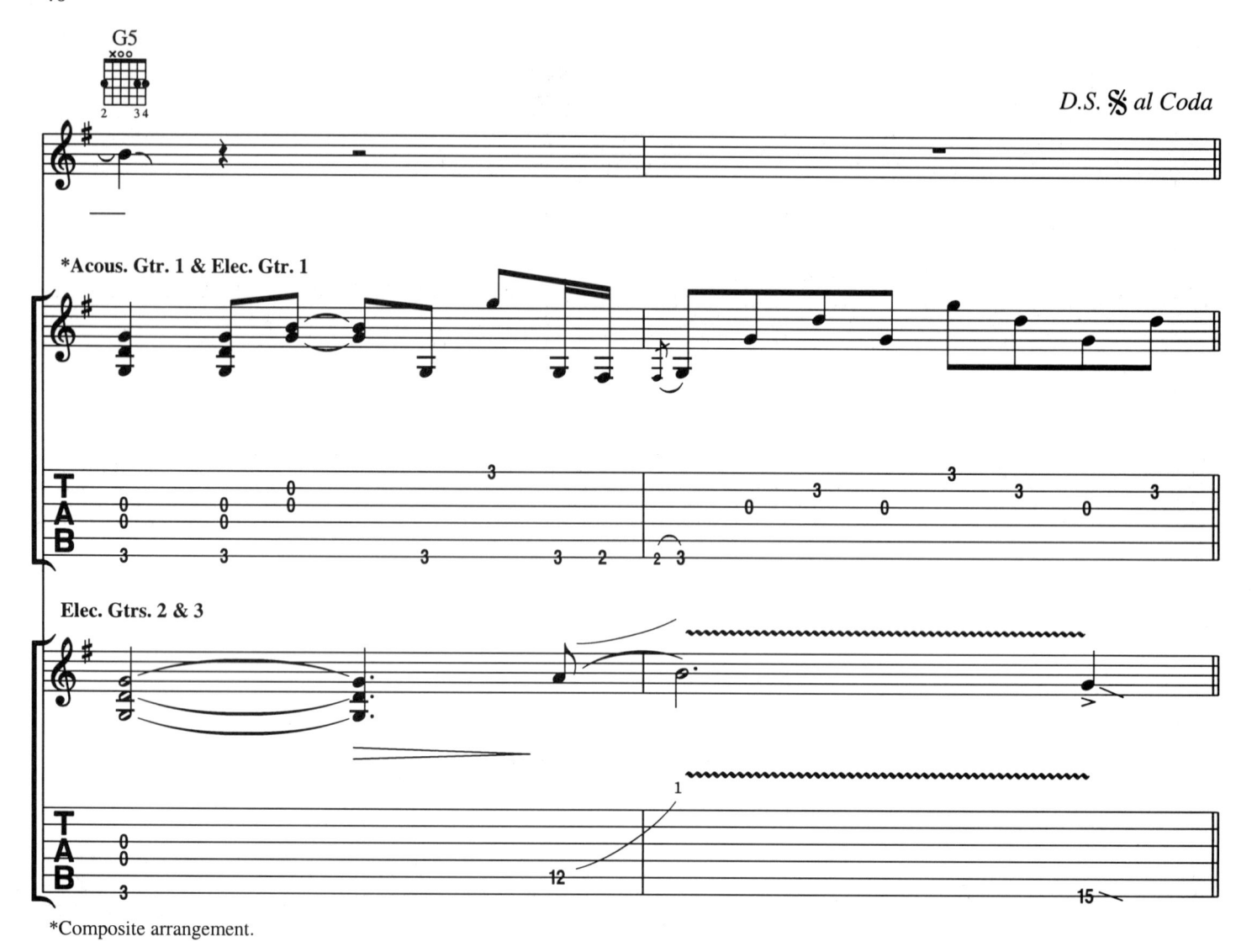

*Composite arrangement.

Bkgd. Vcl.: My brown eyed girl, ___ my brown eyed girl. ___ You ___ my

hold throughout

Brown Eyed Girl – 11 – 8
0467B

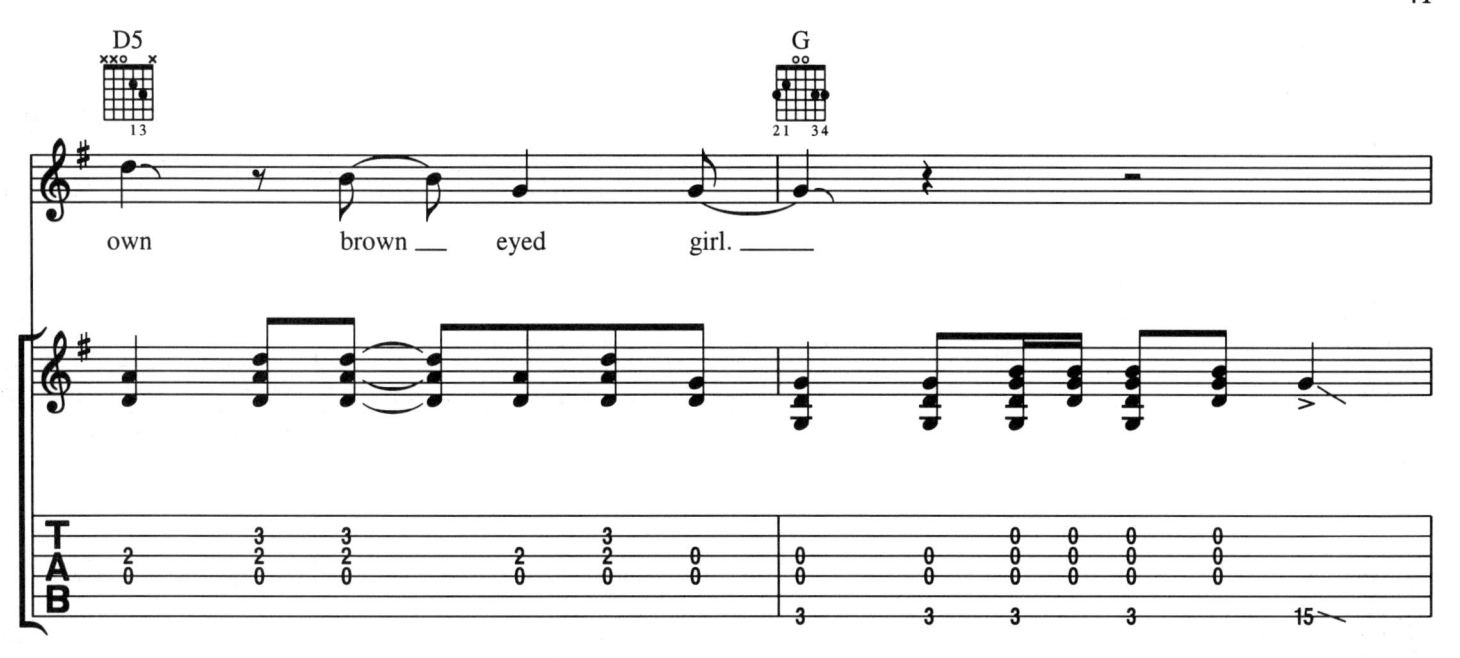

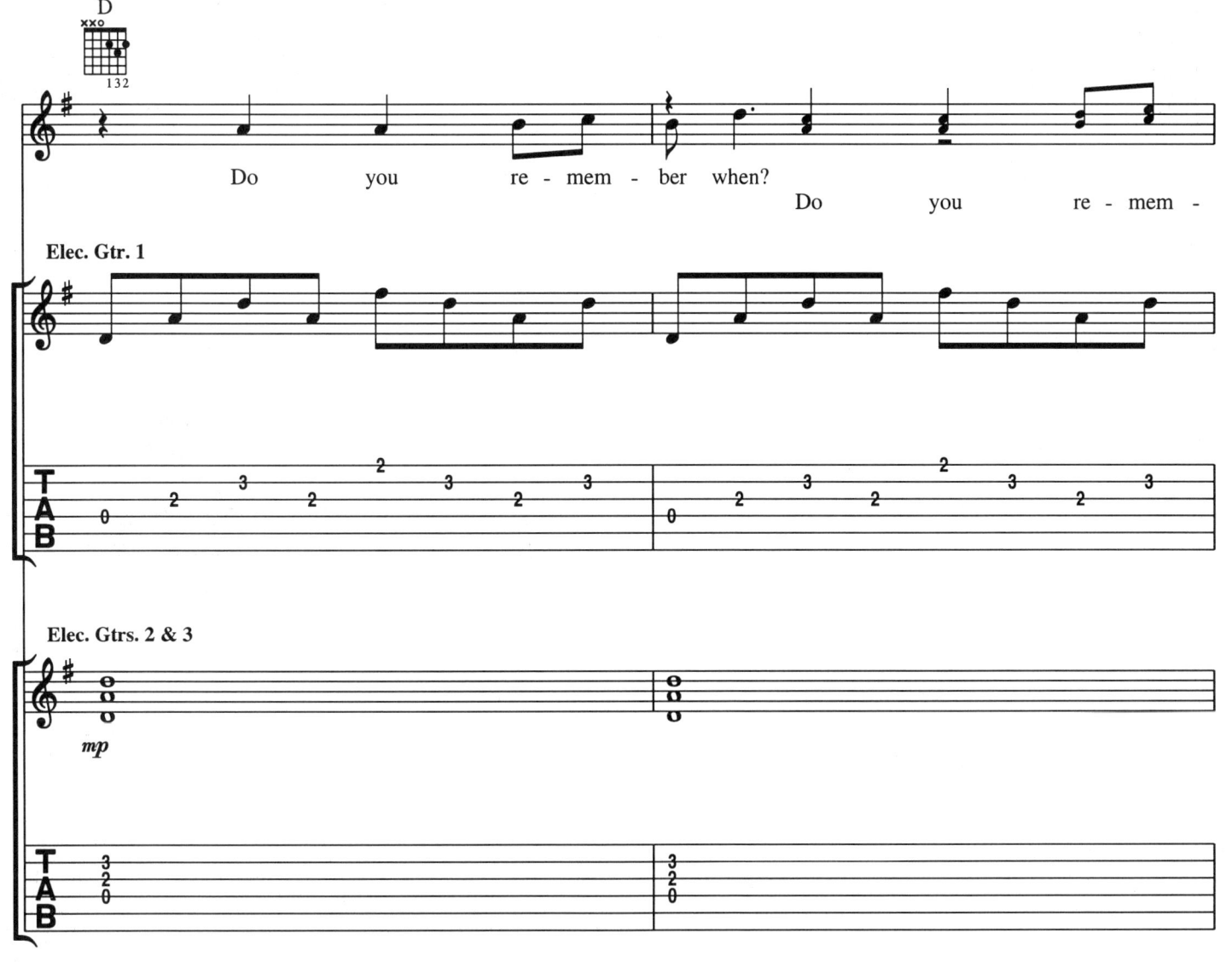

own brown eyed girl.

Do you remember when? Do you remem-

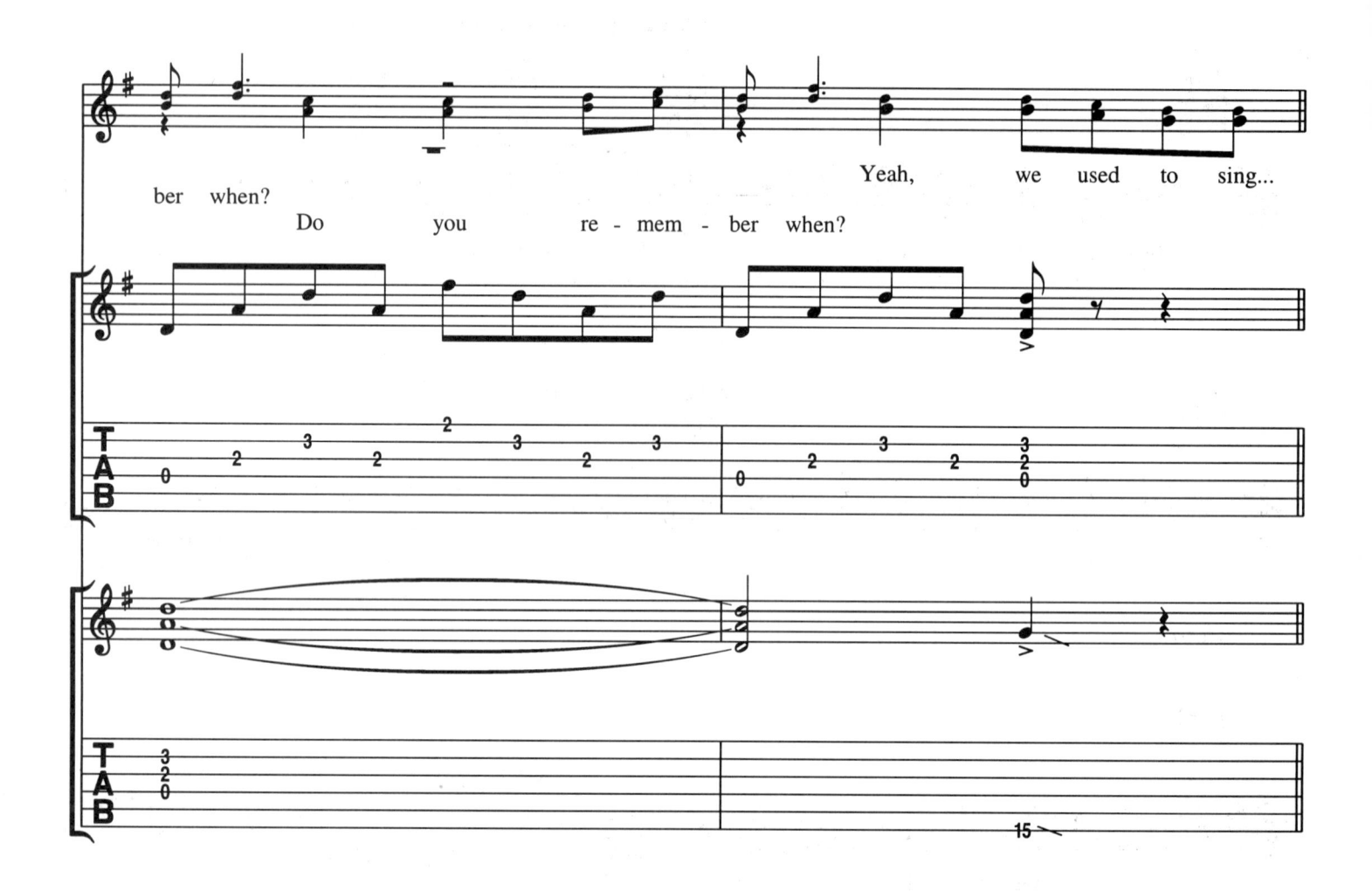

42

ber when? Do you re-mem-ber when? Yeah, we used to sing...

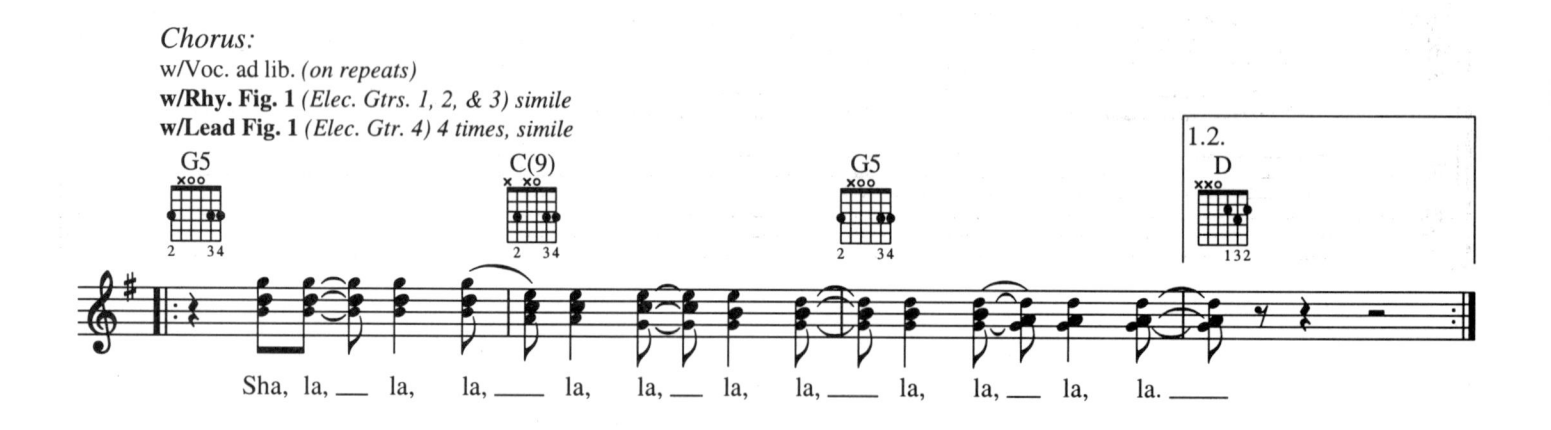

Chorus:
w/Voc. ad lib. *(on repeats)*
w/Rhy. Fig. 1 *(Elec. Gtrs. 1, 2, & 3) simile*
w/Lead Fig. 1 *(Elec. Gtr. 4) 4 times, simile*

G5   C(9)   G5   1.2. D

Sha, la, la, la, la, la, la, la, la, la, la, la.

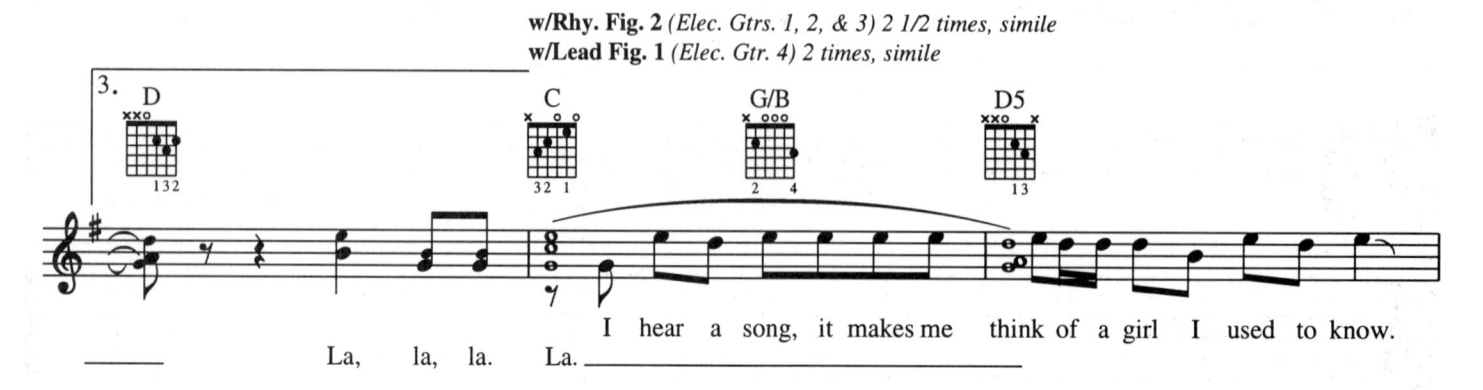

w/Rhy. Fig. 2 *(Elec. Gtrs. 1, 2, & 3) 2 1/2 times, simile*
w/Lead Fig. 1 *(Elec. Gtr. 4) 2 times, simile*

3. D   C   G/B   D5

La, la, la. La. I hear a song, it makes me think of a girl I used to know.

Brown Eyed Girl – 11 – 10
0467B

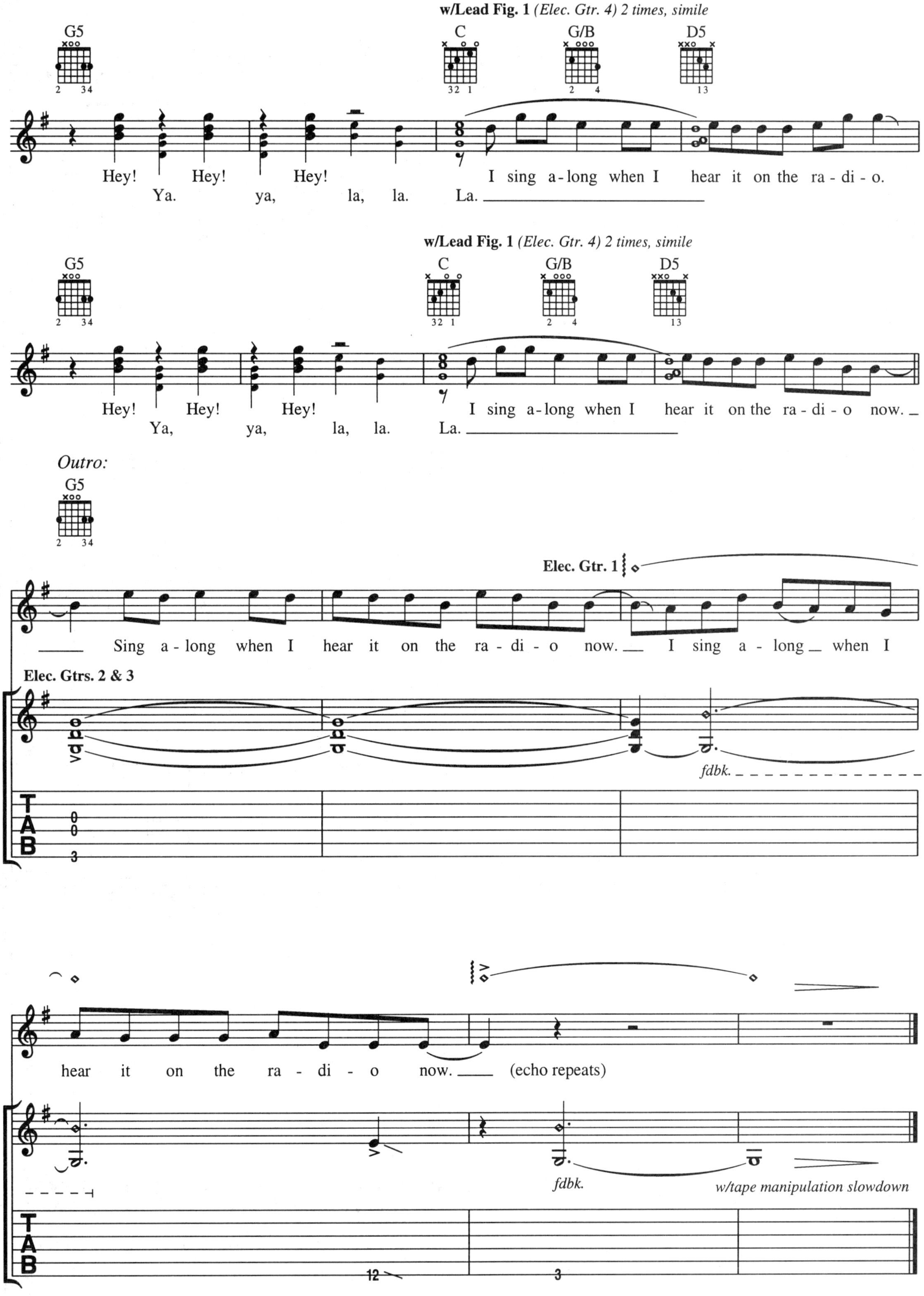
w/Lead Fig. 1 (Elec. Gtr. 4) 2 times, simile
G5
C
G/B
D5
Hey! Hey! Hey! I sing a-long when I hear it on the ra-di-o.
Ya. ya, la, la. La.
w/Lead Fig. 1 (Elec. Gtr. 4) 2 times, simile
G5
C
G/B
D5
Hey! Hey! Hey! I sing a-long when I hear it on the ra-di-o now.
Ya, ya, la, la. La.
Outro:
G5
Elec. Gtr. 1
Sing a-long when I hear it on the ra-di-o now. I sing a-long when I
Elec. Gtrs. 2 & 3
fdbk.
hear it on the ra-di-o now. (echo repeats)
fdbk.
w/tape manipulation slowdown

LEARNING HOW TO SMILE

lyrics by alexakis
music by everclear

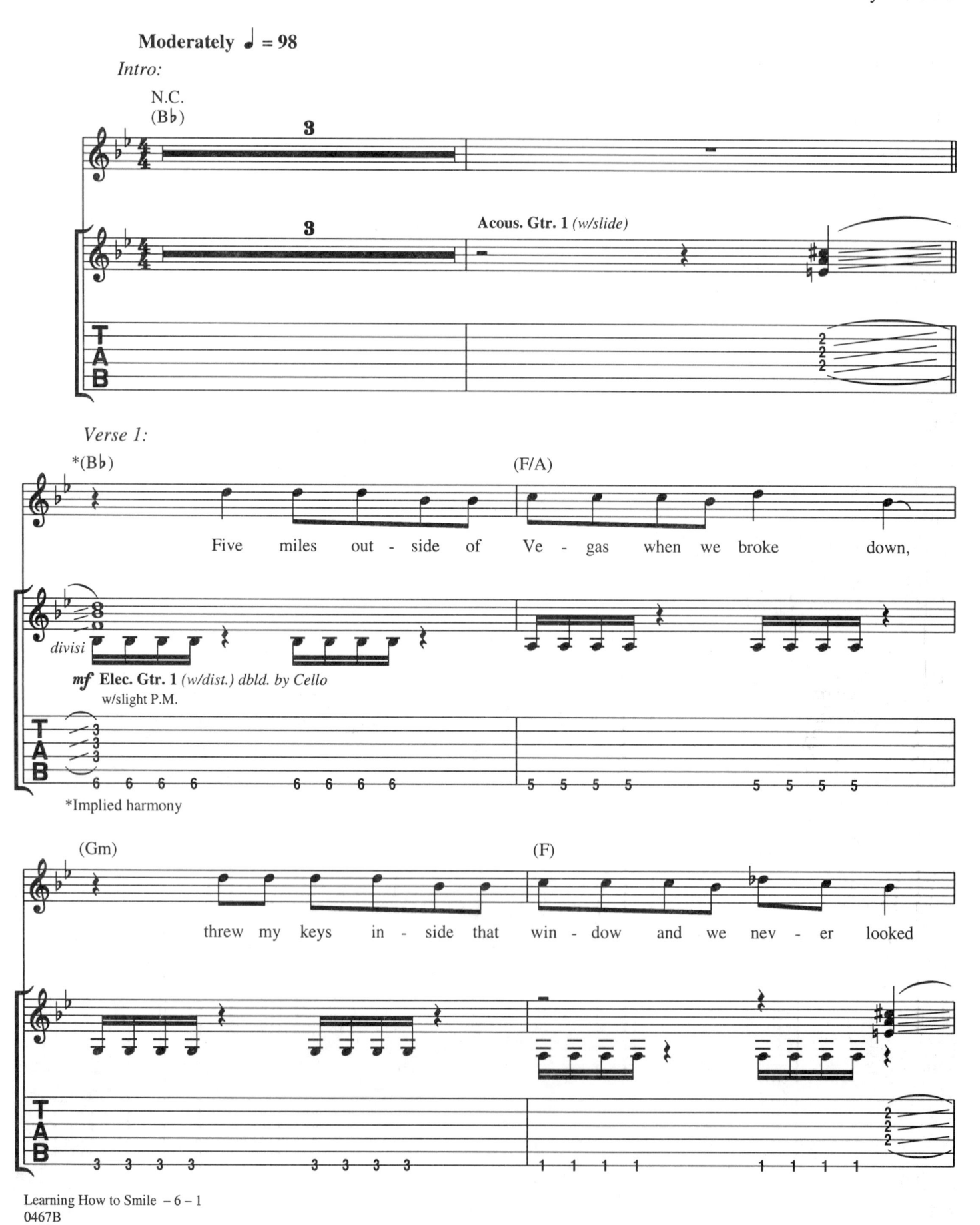

Moderately ♩ = 98

Intro:

Acous. Gtr. 1 *(w/slide)*

Verse 1:

Five miles outside of Vegas when we broke down,

mf Elec. Gtr. 1 *(w/dist.)* dbld. by Cello
w/slight P.M.

*Implied harmony

threw my keys inside that window and we never looked

Learning How to Smile – 6 – 1
0467B

© 2000 evergleam music / montalupis music / commongreen music / irving music, inc. (BMI)
all rights reserved

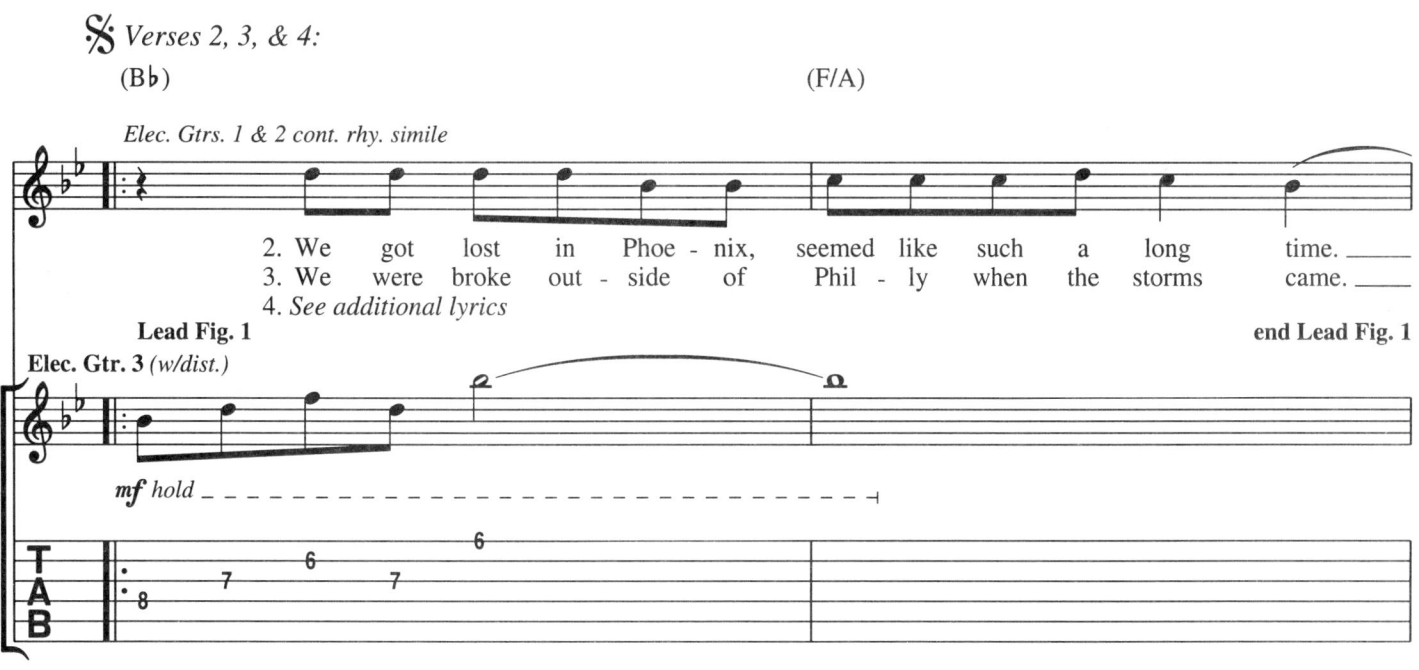

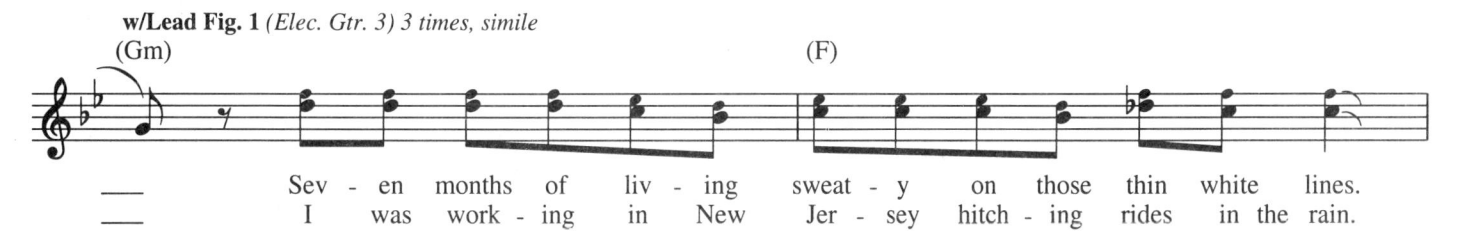

back. We got all drunk and sloppy on a Greyhound bus. We passed out cold so all them losers, they were laughing at us. I will never let them break your heart. I will never let them break me.

%: Verses 2, 3, & 4:

2. We got lost in Phoenix, seemed like such a long time.
3. We were broke outside of Philly when the storms came.
4. *See additional lyrics*

Seven months of living sweaty on those thin white lines.
I was working in New Jersey hitching rides in the rain.

Learning How to Smile – 6 – 2
0467B

46

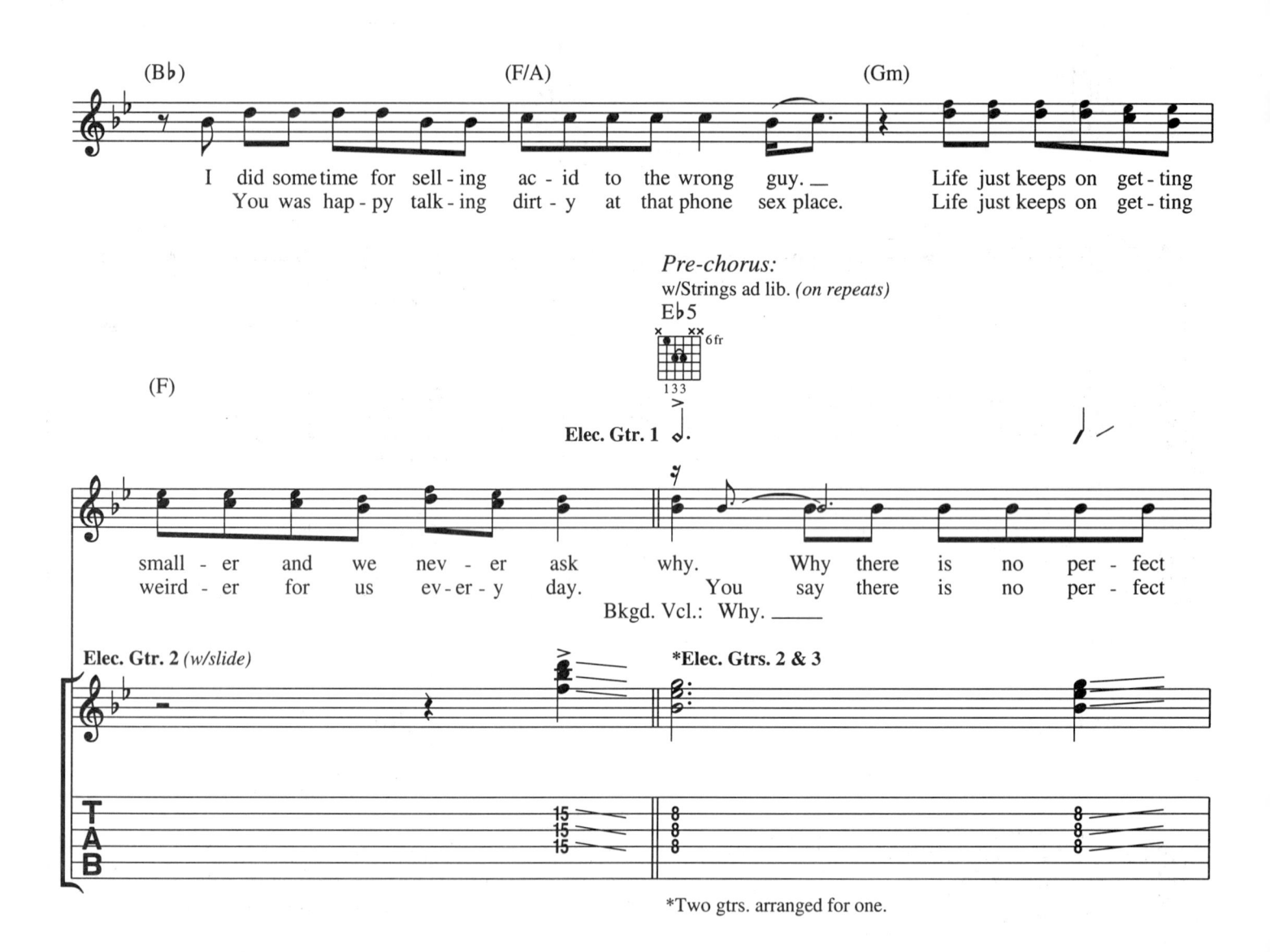

(Bb)　　　　　　　　　(F/A)　　　　　　　　(Gm)

I did some time for sell-ing ac-id to the wrong guy. __ Life just keeps on get-ting
You was hap-py talk-ing dirt-y at that phone sex place. Life just keeps on get-ting

Pre-chorus:
w/Strings ad lib. *(on repeats)*

Eb5

(F)

Elec. Gtr. 1

small - er and we nev - er ask why. Why there is no per - fect
weird - er for us ev - er - y day. You say there is no per - fect
Bkgd. Vcl.: Why. ___

Elec. Gtr. 2 *(w/slide)*　　　　　　　　*Elec. Gtrs. 2 & 3

*Two gtrs. arranged for one.

F5　　　　Bb5　　　F/A　　　G5　　　F5　　　*To Coda* ⊕

place, yes, I know this is true. __ I'm just learn-ing how to smile and that's not eas - y to do. __
place, I say I know this is true. __ We are just learn-ing how to smile and that's not eas - y to do. __

hold _ _ _ _ _ _ _ _ _ _ _ _ _

Learning How to Smile – 6 – 3
0467B

E♭5
1.
F5
I know there will come a day, when we can leave and just go
We both live for the day,
hold
B♭5
2.
F5
Bkgd. run-ning a-way. Oo, yeah. when we can run a-way.
Vcl.: Run-ning a-way.
Chorus:
w/Bkgd. Vcl. Fig. 1, 3 times, simile
B♭5 B5 C5 C♯5 D5 E♭5 D5 C5 B♭5 B5 C5 C♯5
Elec. Gtrs. 1 & 3
Cont. rhy. simile
Bkgd. Vcl. Fig. 1
end Bkgd. Vcl. Fig. 1
Oh, ba-by, we can leave and run a-way. Yes, we can
Hey! Hey! Hey! Hey!

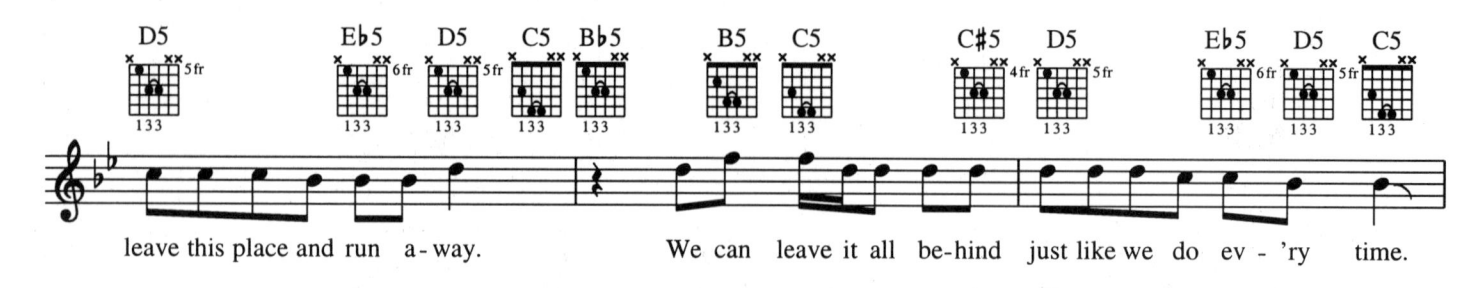

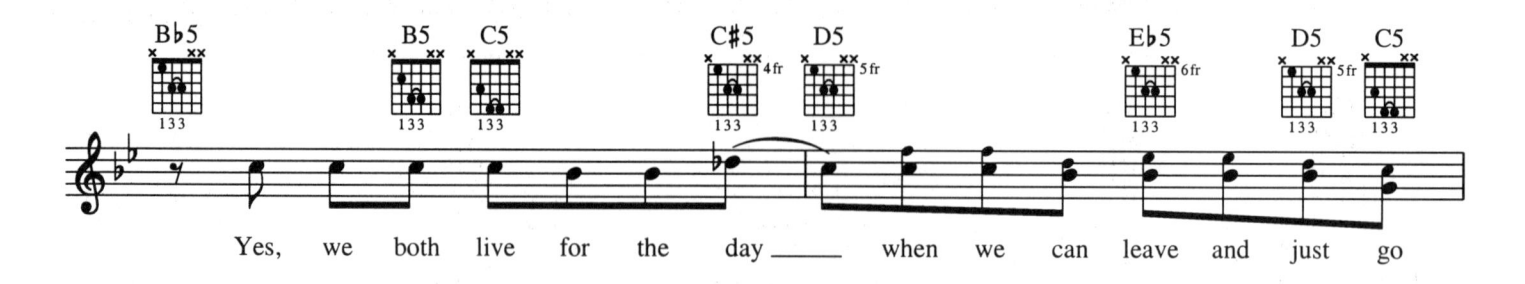

leave this place and run a-way. We can leave it all be-hind just like we do ev-'ry time.

Yes, we both live for the day ___ when we can leave and just go

run-ning a-way. ___ No, I will nev-er let it break your heart.

No, I will nev-er let it break me.

D.S. al Coda

Learning How to Smile – 6 – 5
0467B

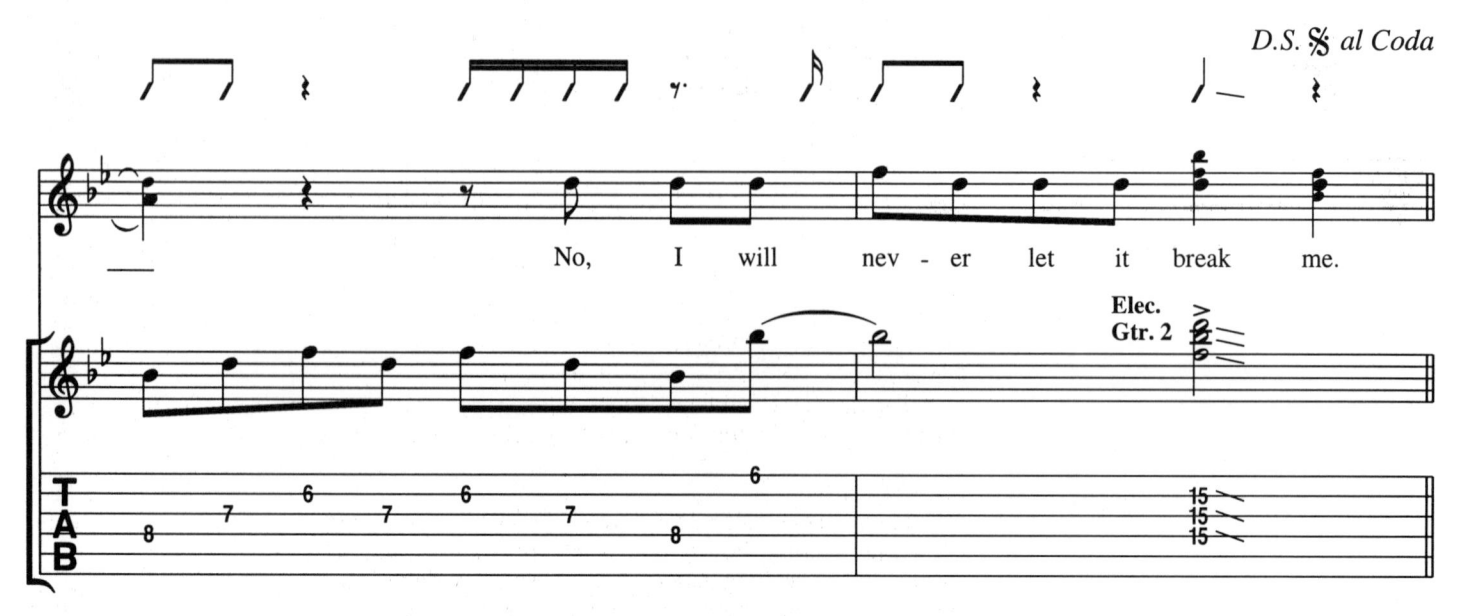

Verse 4:
Five miles outside of Vegas, five years down the line,
We got married in the desert, in the sunshine.
I can handle all the hell that happens everyday,
When you smile and touch my face you make it all just go away.

Pre-chorus:
Yes, I know there ain't no finish line, I know this never ends.
We are just learning how to fall and climb back up again.
I know there is nothing perfect, I know there is nothing new.
We are just learning how to live together, me and you.
(To Chorus:)

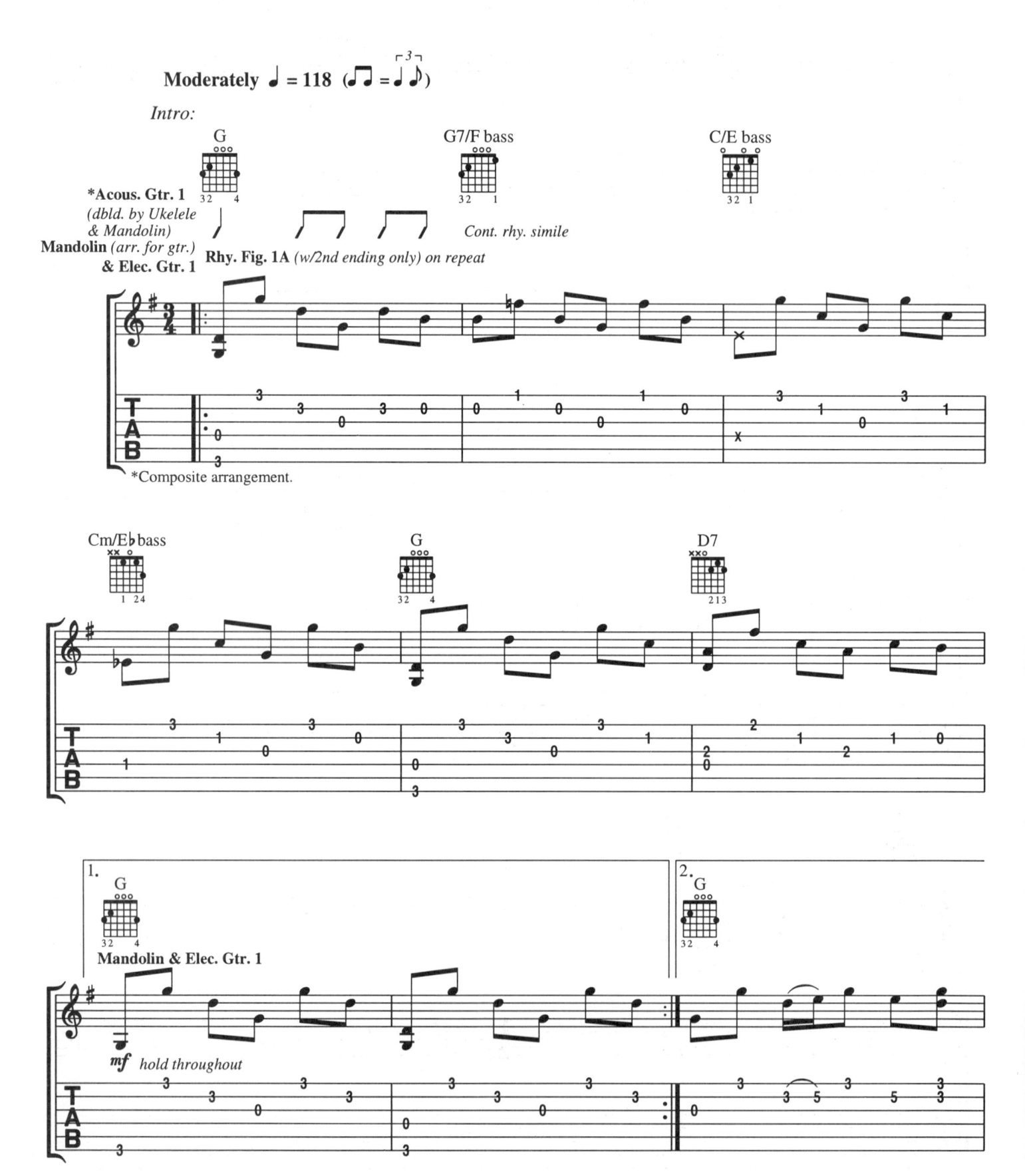

THE HONEYMOON SONG

lyrics by eklund
music by everclear

All Gtrs. Capo V

Moderately ♩ = 118

Chorus:
C
D
Acous. Gtr. 1,
Ukelele (arr. for gtr.), & Mandolin
Cont. rhy. simile
You know I love you, ba -
end Rhy. Fig. 1A
G
C
- by, and I know you love
Mandolin
D
G
me too. But the fun

To Coda
C
D
G
C
that day didn't start un - til we
Interlude:
w/Rhy. Fig. 1A (Mandolin) 1st 6 bars only
D
G
left on our hon - ey - moon.
Elec. Gtr. 1
G7/F bass
C/E bass
Cm/E♭bass
G
Cont. rhy. simile
D7
G
We
Mandolin
mf

Verse 1:

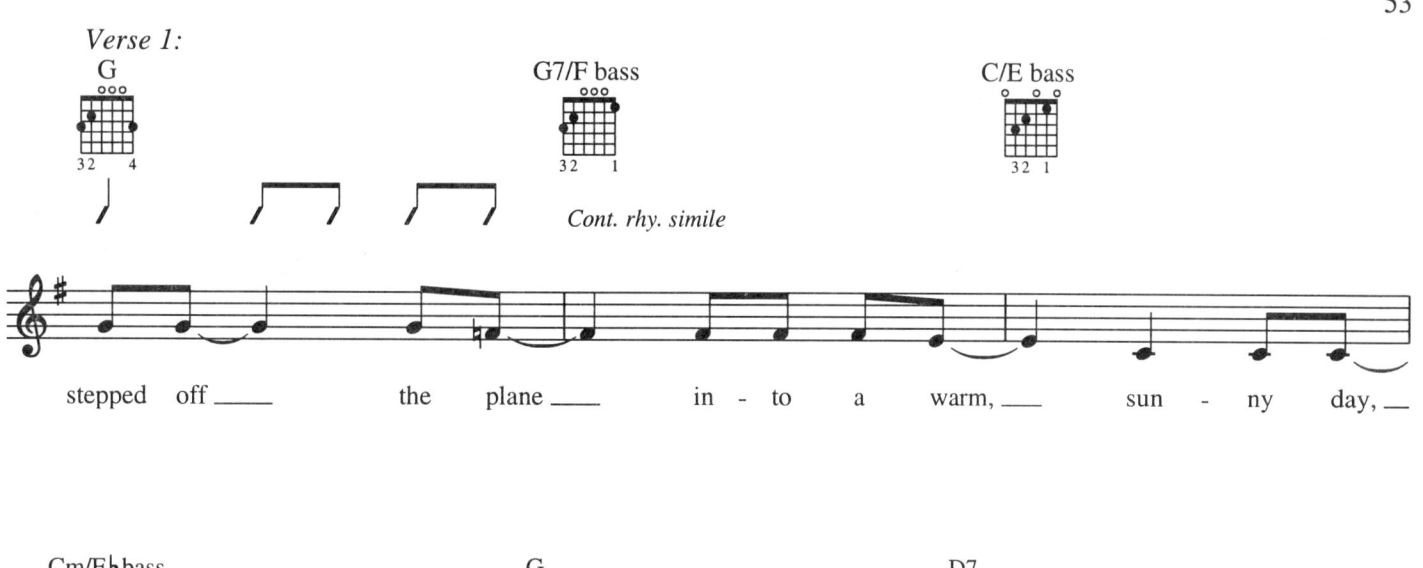

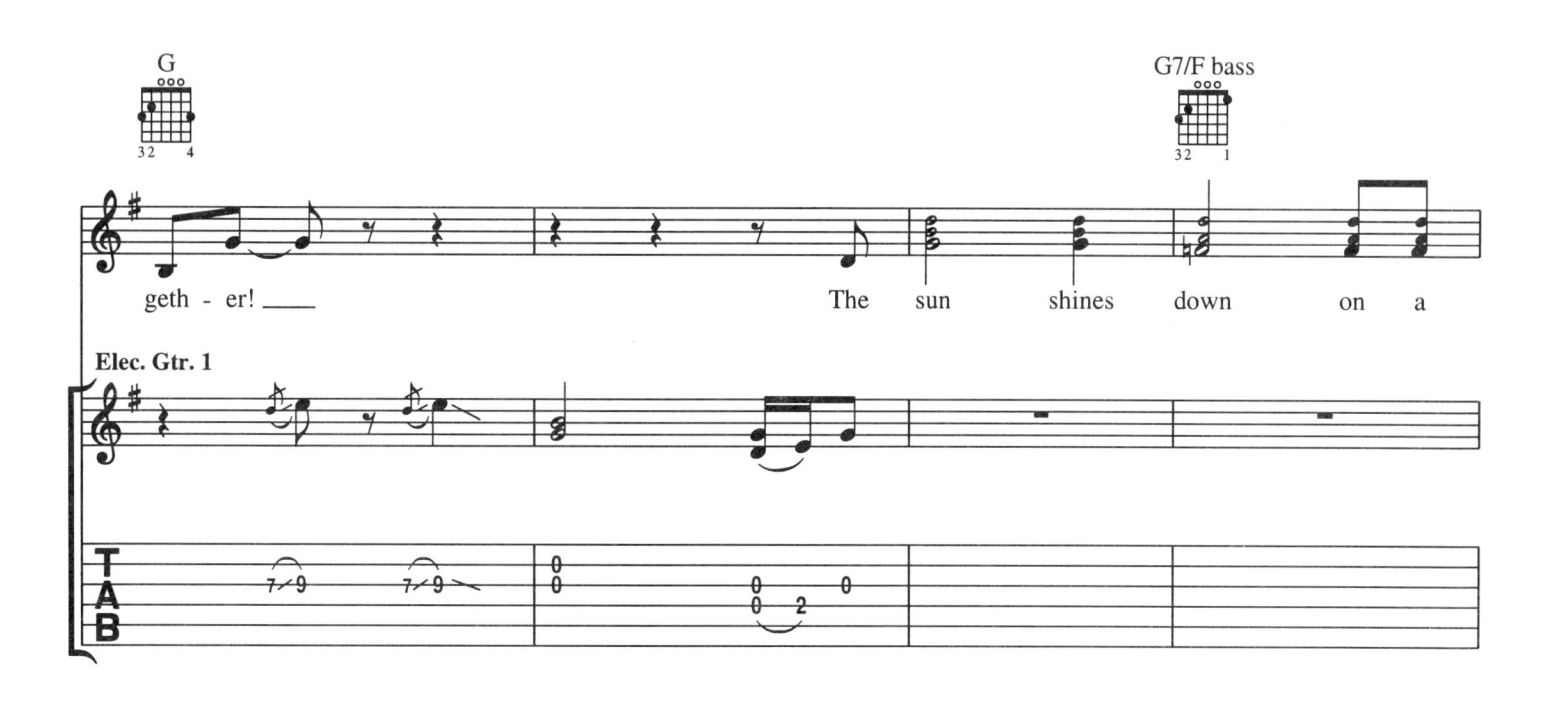

stepped off ___ the plane ___ in - to a warm, ___ sun - ny day, ___ then we ___ got leid ___ to - geth - er! ___ The sun shines down on a Han - a lei town, ___ where the fish ___ all ___ smile ___ 'cause they

The Honeymoon Song – 9 – 4
0467B

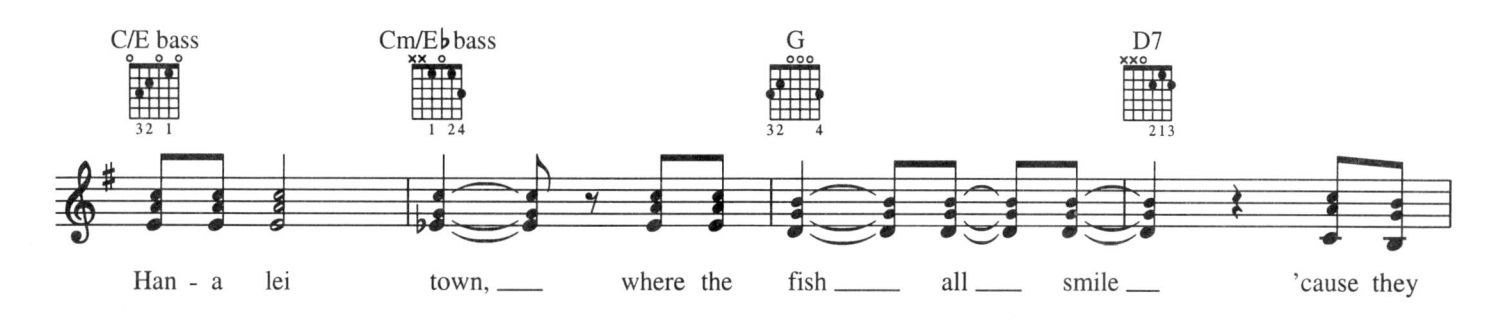

G
C
D
Cont. rhy. simile
know us. Our wed - ding day was warm
Mandolin
Lead Fig. 1
end Lead Fig. 1
w/Lead Fig. 1 (Mandolin) 2 times, simile
and sun - ny. Our friends and fam - 'ly came from
out of town. We said, "I do," then ate
some food and smiled un - til the sun went down.

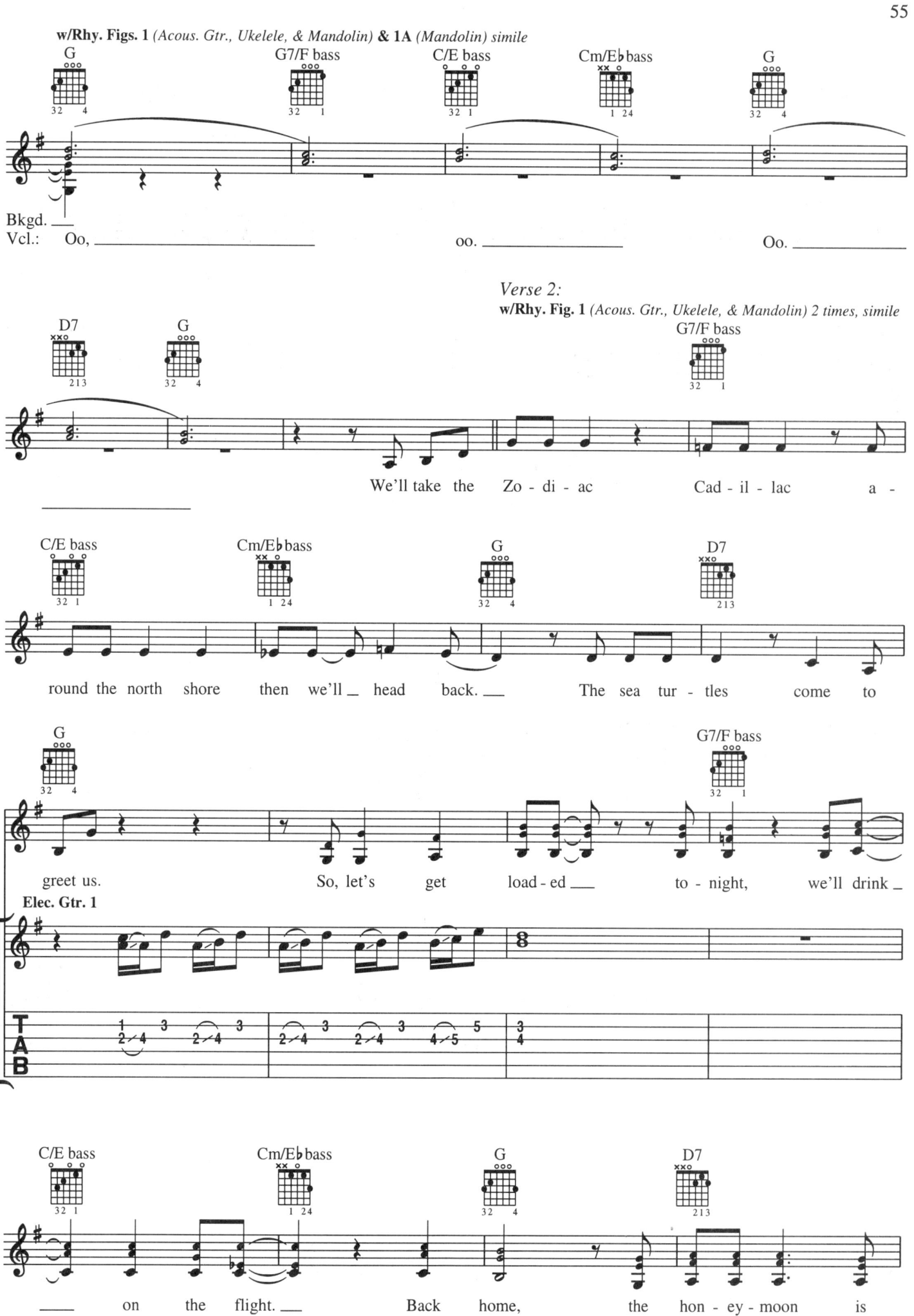

55

w/Rhy. Figs. 1 *(Acous. Gtr., Ukelele, & Mandolin)* **& 1A** *(Mandolin) simile*

Bkgd.
Vcl.: Oo, _____ oo. _____ Oo. _____

Verse 2:
w/Rhy. Fig. 1 *(Acous. Gtr., Ukelele, & Mandolin) 2 times, simile*

We'll take the Zo-di-ac Cad-il-lac a-round the north shore then we'll head back. The sea tur-tles come to greet us. So, let's get load-ed to-night, we'll drink on the flight. Back home, the hon-ey-moon is

Elec. Gtr. 1

The Honeymoon Song – 9 – 6
0467B

G
Solo:
w/Rhy. Fig. 1 (Elec. Gtr. 1, Ukelele, & Mandolin)
o - ver.
Mandolin (dbld.)
G7/F bass
C/E bass
Cm/E♭ bass
1/2
G
D7
G
D.S. 𝄋 al Coda
You know

57

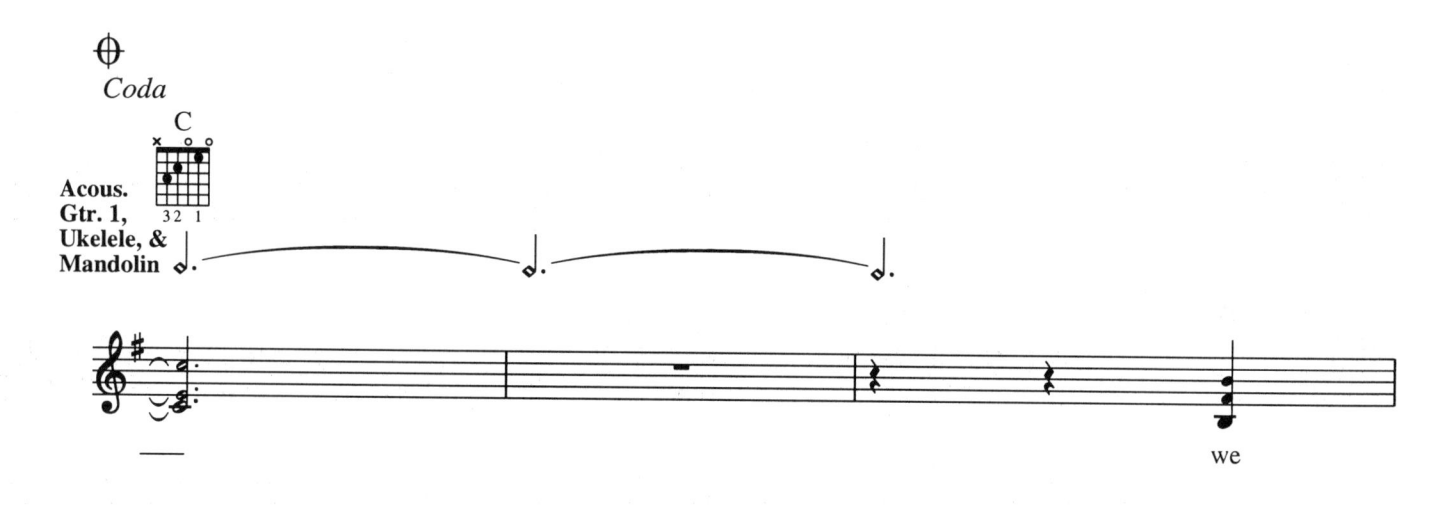

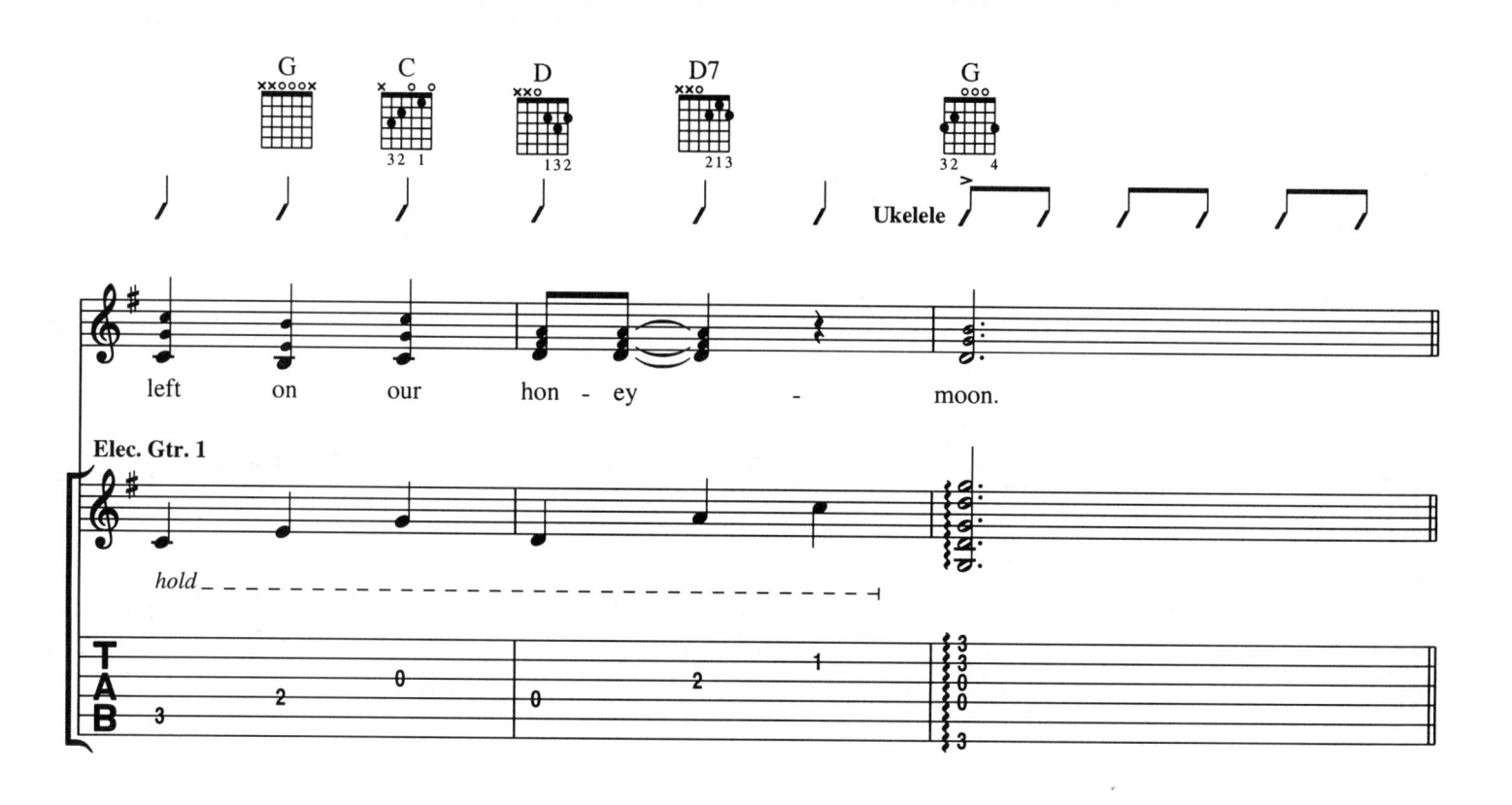

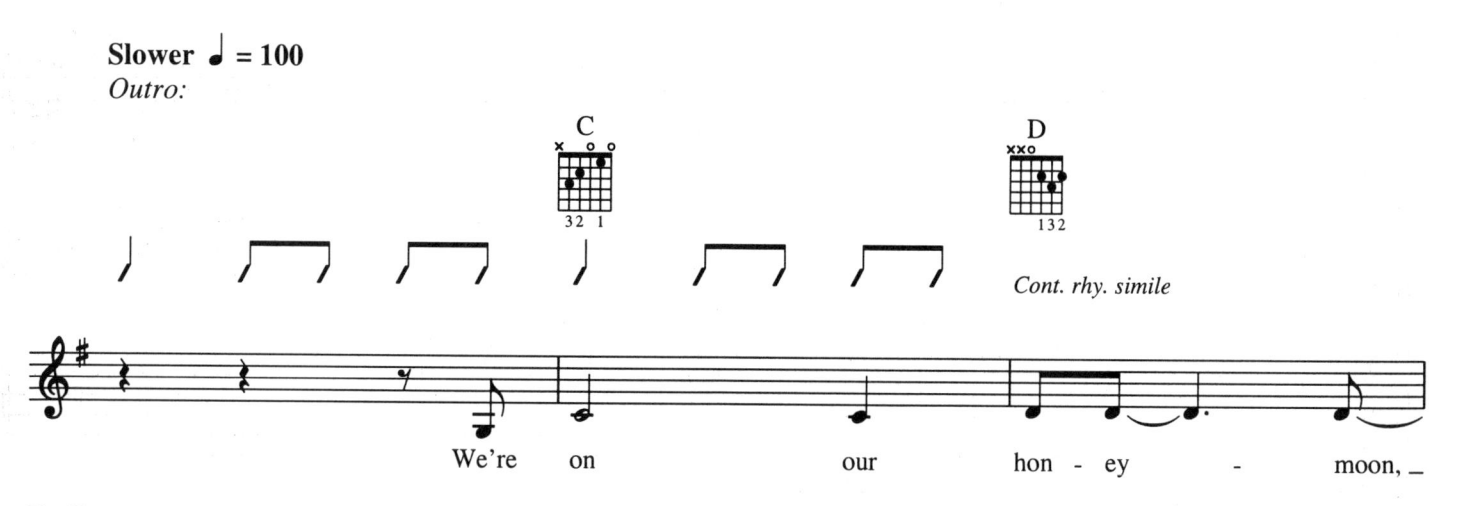

58

we're on our hon - ey - moon. ___ The fun that day ___ did - n't start ___ un - til we left on our hon - ey - moon.

All Instruments

Acous. Gtr. 1, Ukelele, & Mandolin

Elec. Gtr. 1

hold

The Honeymoon Song – 9 – 9
0467B

NOW THAT IT'S OVER

lyrics by alexakis
music by everclear

Slowly ♩ = 68

Intro:

Yeah, right! Spoken: It's over, it's over. One, two,

Verse 1:

three, four. Break-down and shake for me. Nothing ever is the way you want it to be. Nothing even tastes right, now that it's o-

Now That's It's Over – 6 – 1
0467B

© 2000 evergleam music / montalupis music / commongreen music / irving music, inc. (BMI)
all rights reserved

-ver. Break down ___ and shake for me, ___

Bkgd. Vcl.: Oo. ___

Rhy. Fig. 1

___ don't write words un-less you want me to read ___ them. Noth-ing real-ly mat-ters now that it's o-

-ver. (echo repeats) May-be we can be friends ___ now that we're old-er. We can have
Oo, ___

Elec. Gtr. 2 *(dbld. by Elec. Gtr. 1)*

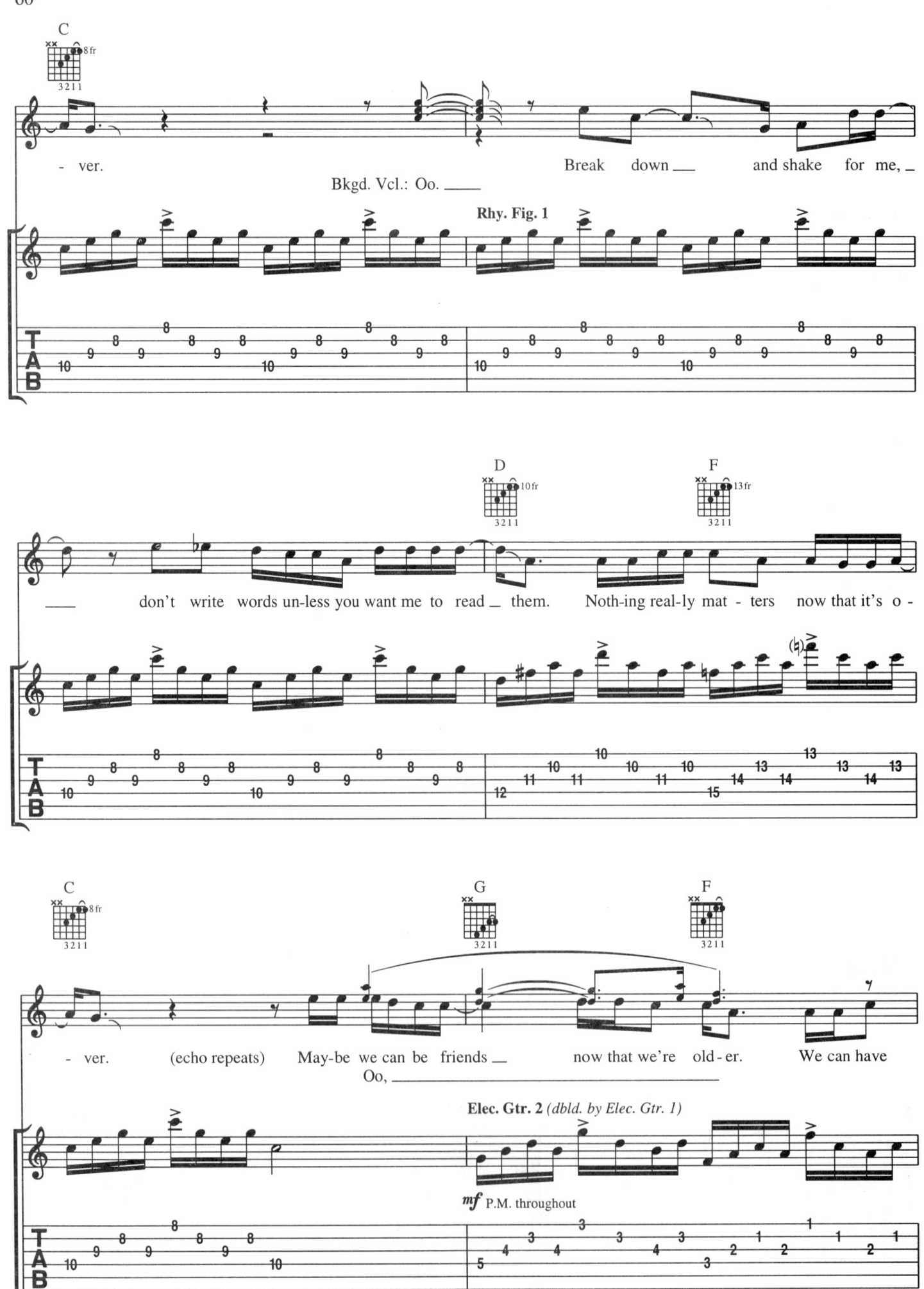

mf P.M. throughout

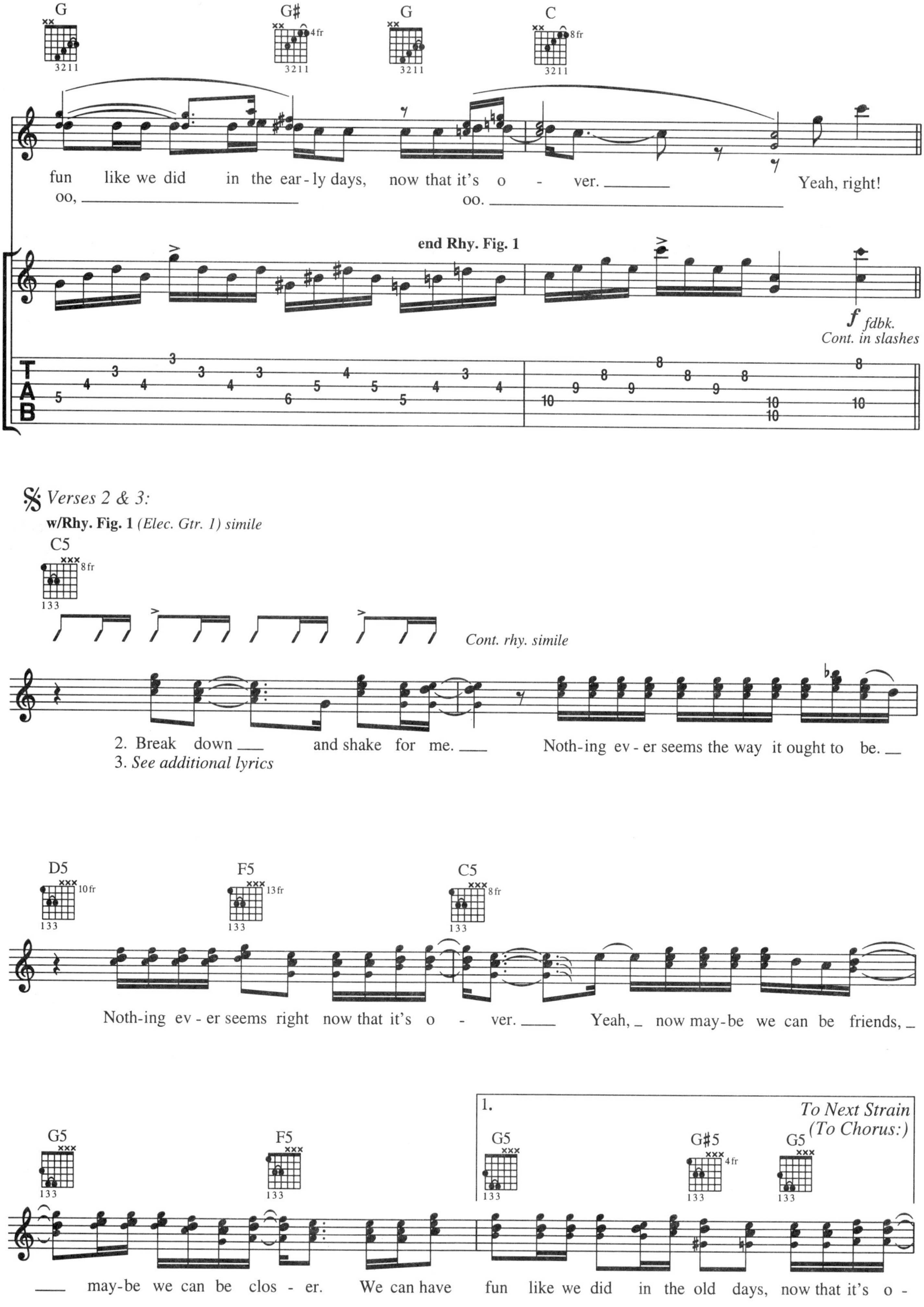
G
G#
G
C
fun like we did in the ear-ly days, now that it's o - ver. Yeah, right!
oo, oo.
end Rhy. Fig. 1
f fdbk.
Cont. in slashes
Verses 2 & 3:
w/Rhy. Fig. 1 (Elec. Gtr. 1) simile
C5
Cont. rhy. simile
2. Break down and shake for me. Noth-ing ev - er seems the way it ought to be.
3. See additional lyrics
D5
F5
C5
Noth-ing ev - er seems right now that it's o - ver. Yeah, now may-be we can be friends,
G5
F5
G5
G#5
G5
To Next Strain (To Chorus:)
may-be we can be clos - er. We can have fun like we did in the old days, now that it's o -

to me, may-be I'm dream-ing. I am a lot bet-ter now than just O. K. May-be I am

Chorus:
just wak-ing up in my own way, now that it's o - ver.

{ 1. Ah, yeah, ah
{ 2. *See additional lyrics*

yeah, ah yeah, ah yeah, ah yeah. My bad dreams just don't seem the same,

ba-by, with-out you. I wish you were will-ing to ac-cept the blame,

yeah, for ev-'ry-thing you do. My night-mares just don't scare me now, ba-by, with-out you. Yeah, yeah.

I wish that I could find the words to tell, to tell, to tell, in the

Now That It's Over – 6 – 4
0467B

best way pos-si-ble, you and your friends to go to hell.____ Yeah, right!

Interlude:

____ to tell ___ (echo repeat) you to po-lite-ly go f*** your-self, yeah, now that it's o-
(echo repeat)

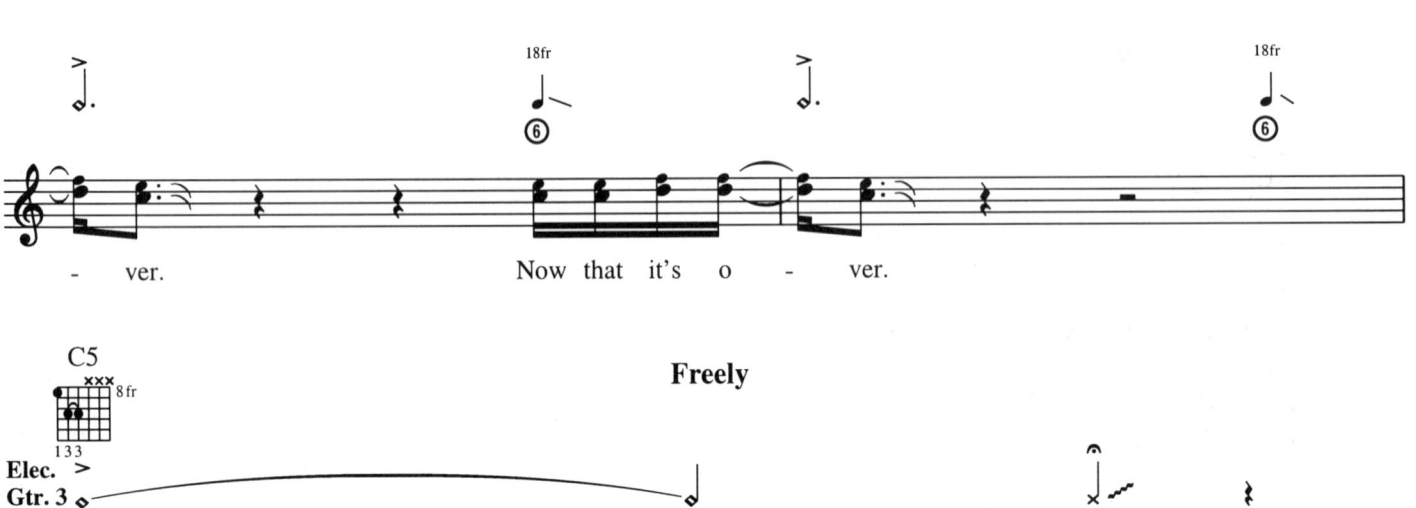

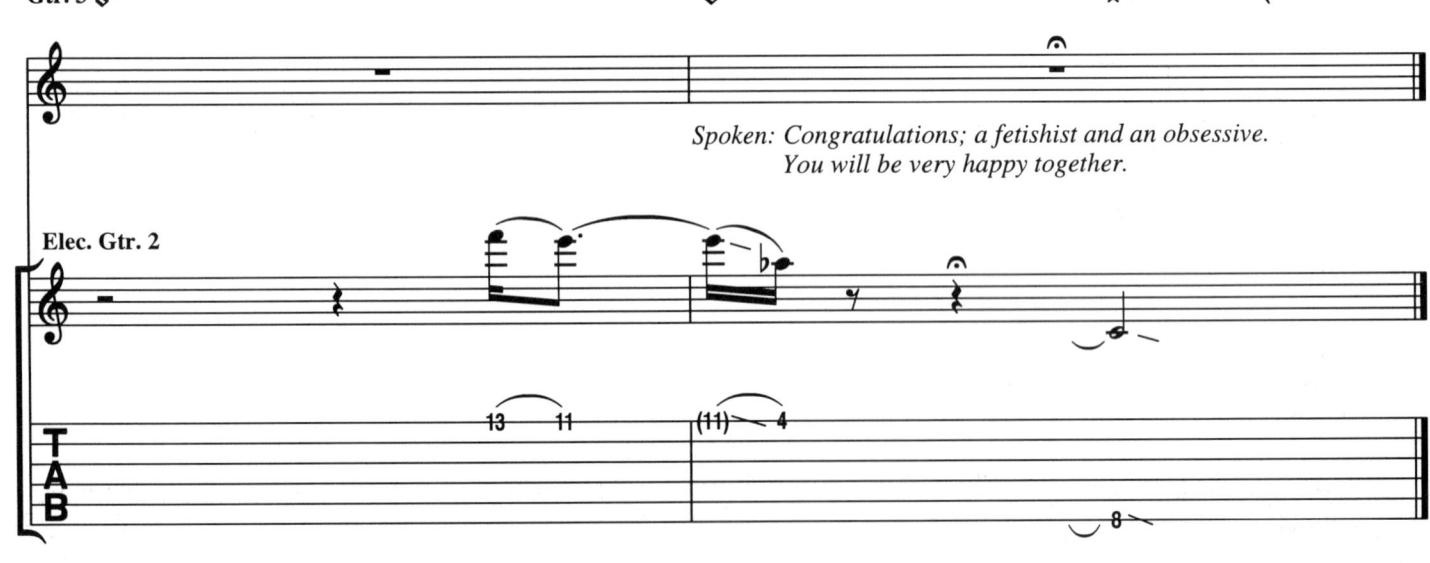

Spoken: Congratulations; a fetishist and an obsessive. You will be very happy together.

Verse 3:
Break up time is never easy to do.
Nothing ever ends the way you want it to.
Nothing seems to make sense
Now that it's over.

Yeah, now maybe we can be friends.
Yeah, now that you're leaving
You can be nice to me.
Maybe I'm dreaming.
I am a lot better now than just OK.
Maybe I am just waking up in my own way
Now that it's over.
(To Chorus:)

Chorus 2:
Now that it's over.
My bad dreams just don't seem the same,
Baby, without you.
I wish you were willing to accept the blame
Yeah, for all the shitty things you do.
Nightmares just don't scare me now,
Baby, without you.
I wish that I could find the words to tell
You to politely go f*** yourself,
Yeah, now that it's over.
(To Outro:)

THRIFT STORE CHAIR

lyrics by alexakis
music by everclear

Moderately ♩ = 84

1. Ba-by, go to bed and put out the light. Oo,
2. Yeah, I wish we'd nev-er bought a king-size bed. Yeah,

*Acous. Gtr. 1 (dbld. by 12-string acous.)

mf hold throughout

*Composite arrangement.

we both know if we talk an-y-more we are go-ing to end up in a great big fight.
the on-ly damn thing that it's ev-er been good for, is plen-ty room for the real good sex.

Thrift Store Chair – 6 – 1
0467B

© 2000 evergleam music / montalupis music / commongreen music / irving music, inc. (BMI)
all rights reserved

You can have your way a-gain, _ yeah, _ you be-lieve what you want to be-lieve. _
I lay in bed in the dark and all _ that I can see, _ yeah, _

You can walk all o-ver me to-mor-row, but to-night can't we both just pre-tend to sleep? _
is the dis-tance that grows be-tween us. Yeah, you seem so far from me.

Chorus:

I think we're head-ed for a big _ fall, _ I think we're head-ed for a bad time. _
Yes, I think we're head-ed for a real big fall, _ I think we're head-ed for a bad time. _

Bkgd.
Vcl.: Oo, _____ oo,

Thrift Store Chair – 6 – 2
0467B

G
C
G
C
Oo, I'm go-ing to go down-stairs and sit in that chair you like.
Yeah, I'm go-ing to go down-stairs, I'm go-ing to sit by my-self all a-lone in the mid-dle of the
ah.
Am
C
I want to put a John Prine rec-ord on, yes, I need to slow down for a-
night. I'm going to put a John Prine rec-ord on, I think we need to slow down for a-
Oo, oo.
Elec. Gtr. 1 (clean-tone)
mp

Thrift Store Chair – 6 – 4

(echo repeats) I'm gon-na put a John Prine rec-ord on, I think we need to slow down for a-

Outro:

while. _____ While, yeah. _____ We need to slow down for a-

while. _____ While, yeah. _____ We need to slow down for a-

G C G C
while, _ for a - while. ___ Yeah, ___ yeah, we need to slow down for a -
For a-while, for a-while, for a - while. _
G C G C G
while. ___
Elec. Gtr. 1

OTIS REDDING

lyrics by alexakis
music by everclear

Slowly ♩ = 62

Acous. Gtr. 1 (dbld. by 12-string acous.)

mf hold throughout

Composite arrangement.

Verse:

1. Do you re-mem-ber _ when we _ were hun-gry? _ Do you re-mem-ber _ when we _ were cold? _
2. Yeah, do you re-mem-ber _ when we were the los-ers? Do you re-mem-ber _ when we were the lame? _
3. *See additional lyrics*

Rhy. Fig. 1

_ Do you re-mem-ber _ when we _ were hap-py? Do you re-mem-ber, do you re-mem-
_ Do you re-mem-ber _ when we were the lov-ers? Do you re-mem-ber, do you re-mem-

end Rhy. Fig. 1

Otis Redding – 6 – 1
0467B

© 2000 evergleam music / montalupis music / commongreen music / irving music, inc. (BMI)
all rights reserved

72

ber? Do you re-mem-ber _ when we _ were luck-y, we were liv-ing the life _ al-most ev-er-y night. _
ber? Do you re-mem-ber _ when we _ were strung out, eat-ing Top Ram-en and mac-a-ro-ni and cheese? _

I would wrap _ you in _ my thin _ white arms, _ we'd sit and watch the stars die. _
We would get _ so lost _ in that base-

Ay, _ ay, ay, ay, ay, ay, ay, ay, ay, ay, ay, ay.

Otis Redding – 6 – 2
0467B

2.
To Next Strain
(To Chorus:)
A7
C
A7
Cmaj7
- ment room _ and let the O - tis Red-ding sing us to sleep. _ I wish I had one more life.
3.
C
D(11)
D♯+
Am
C
- py? In a way, no one out-side could ev - er know. I wish I had one more life,
Chorus:
Am
C
G5
D(11)
A9
Csus2
how I wish I had one more life to live. I don't want to be wast - ed (echo repeat)

74

I don't want to live in-side this day-dream an-y more. I just want to be hap-py a-gain.

I don't want to be wast-ed, I don't want to be blind. I don't want to be wast-ed, _____

*Implied harmony.

I don't want to live in-side this day-dream an-y more. I just want to be hap-py a-gain.

Otis Redding – 6 – 4
0467B

75

Verse 3:
I wish I could be like all my heroes.
I wish I could be like all yours too.
I wish I could sing like Otis Redding.
I wish I could play this guitar in tune.
Do you remember when we were hungry?
Do you remember when we were cold?
Do you remember when we were happy
In a way, no one outside could ever know?
I wish I had one more life,
How I wish I had one more life to live.
(To Chorus:)

UNEMPLOYED BOYFRIEND

lyrics by alexakis
music by everclear

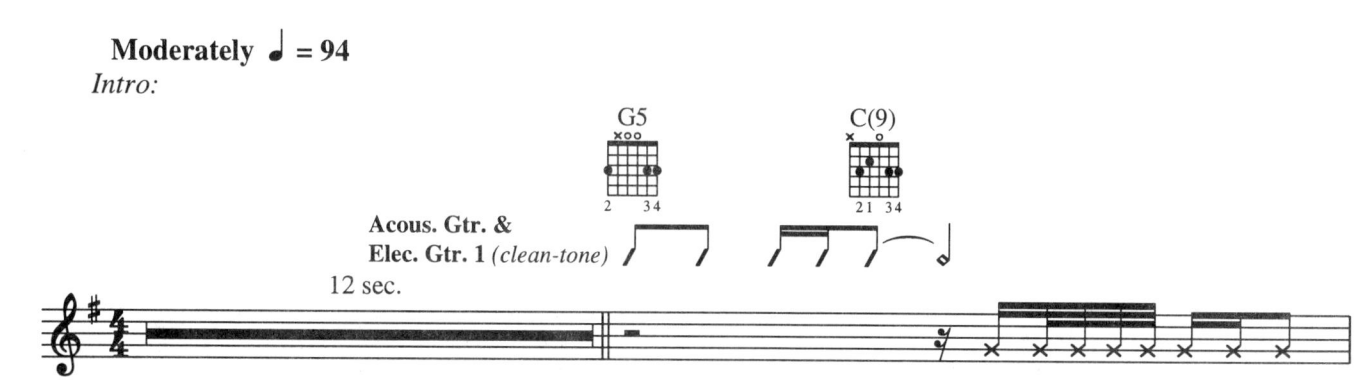

Moderately ♩ = 94
Intro:

**Acous. Gtr. &
Elec. Gtr. 1** *(clean-tone)*
12 sec.

Spoken: Hi, this is Peggy. Leave me a nice message
or I'll kill ya.
2nd voice: Hey, Peggy, it's me. You are never going to
believe what happened to me today.

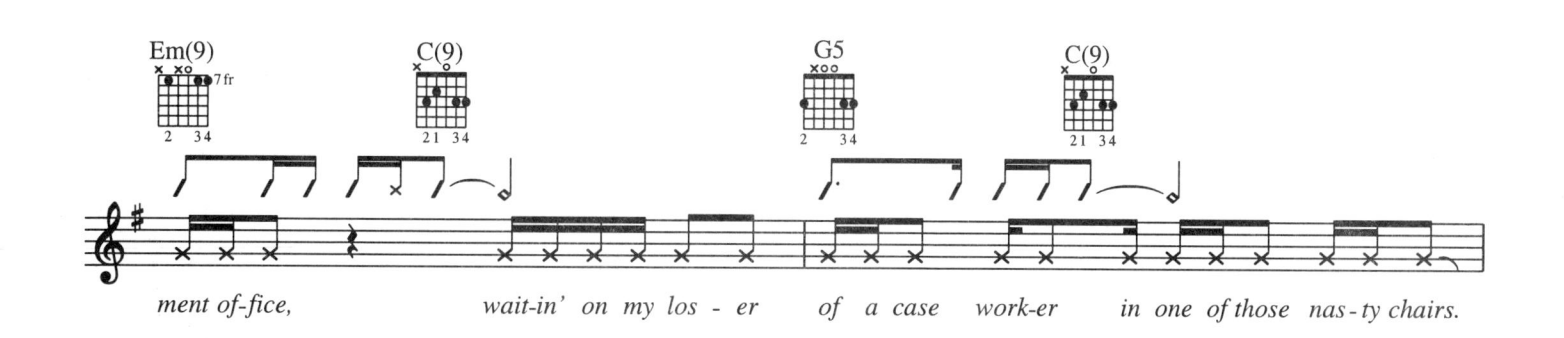

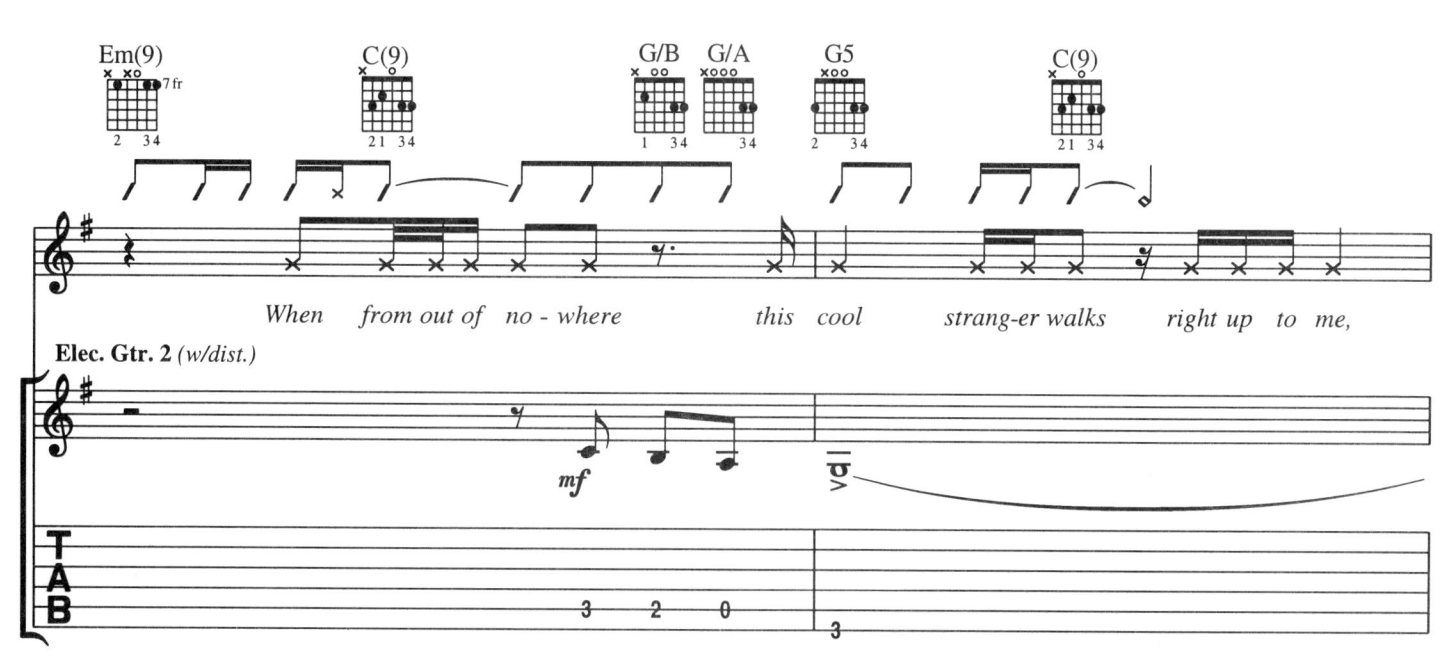

I'm sit-tin' at the un - em - ploy - ment of-fice, wait-in' on my los - er of a case work-er in one of those nas-ty chairs.

When from out of no - where this cool strang-er walks right up to me,

Elec. Gtr. 2 *(w/dist.)*

Unemployed Boyfriend – 11 – 1
0467B

© 2000 evergleam music / montalupis music / commongreen music / irving music, inc. (BMI)
all rights reserved

sits down, then leans o-ver and says some-thing like, "This is gon-na sound a lit-tle ob-ses-sive..." (echo repeats)

Verses 1 & 2:

1. This is going to sound a lit-tle ob-ses-sive, this is going to sound a lit-tle bit strange.
2. that ev-er since I first saw you sit-ting on your car out-side.

Elec. Gtr. 3 *(clean-tone) on repeat*

Lead Fig. 1 ... **end Lead Fig. 1**

mp harm.
hold

Unemployed Boyfriend – 11 – 2
0467B

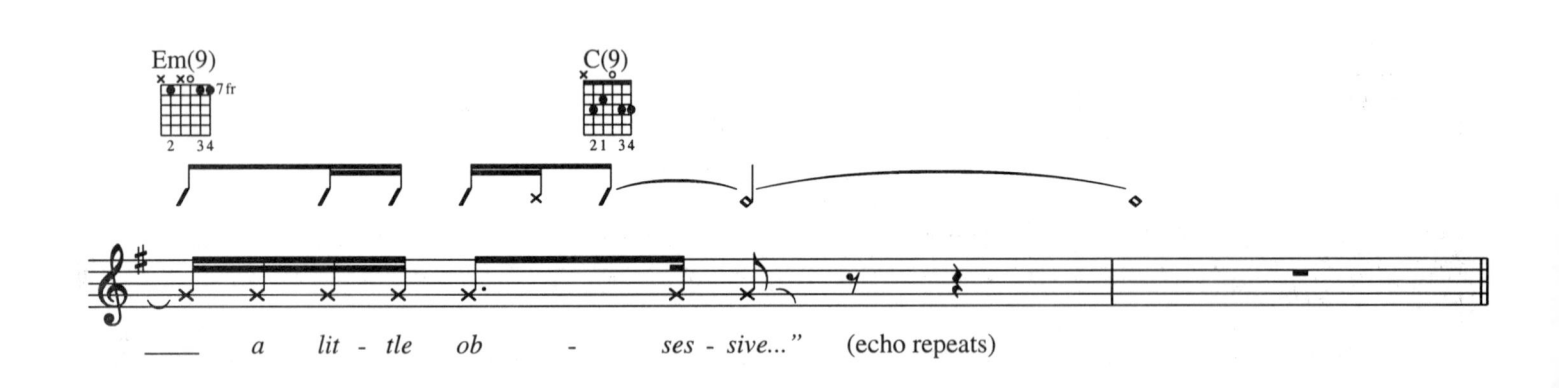

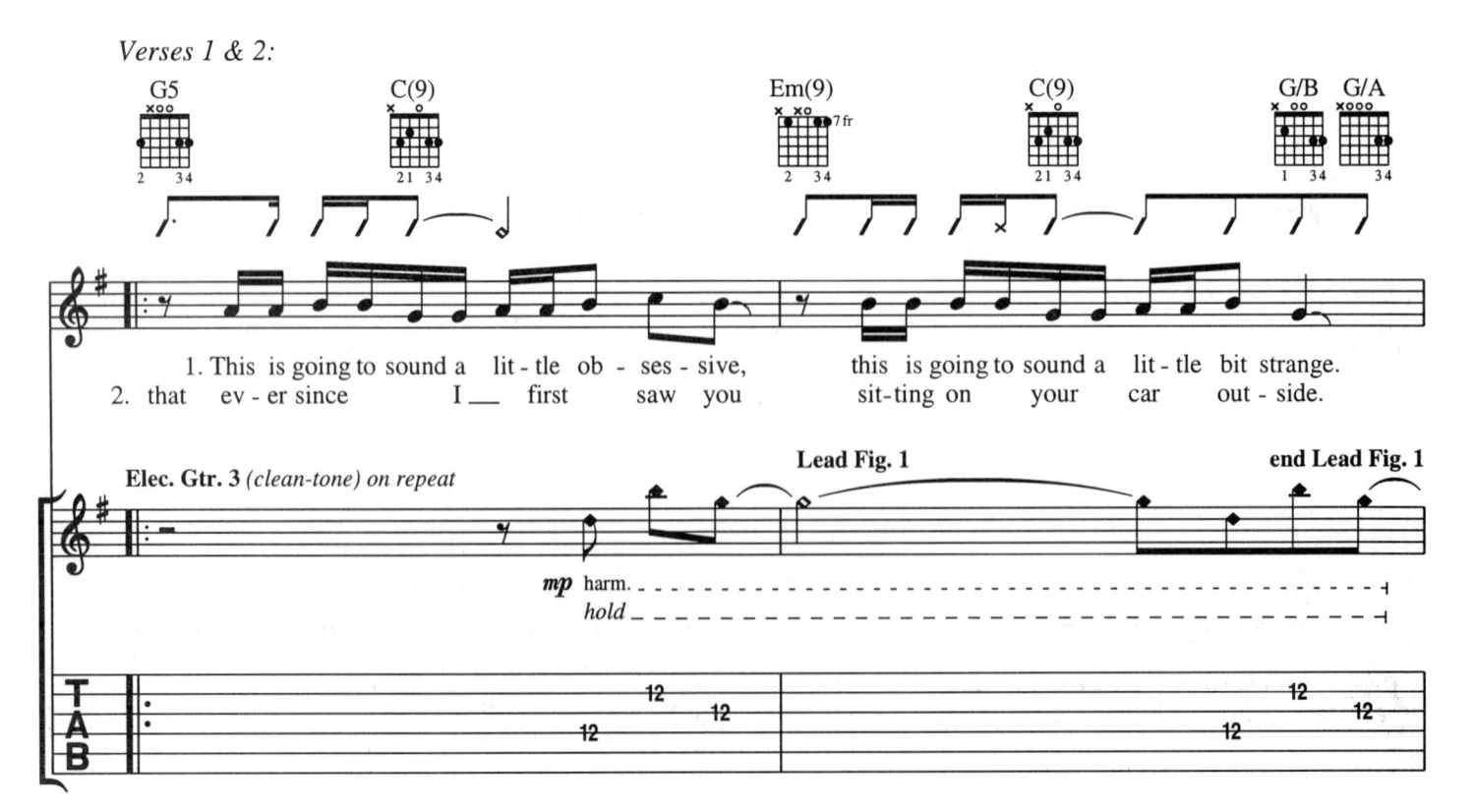

w/Lead Fig. 1 *(Elec. Gtr. 3) 6 times, simile*

Cont. rhy. simile

I have one thing to say before I turn and I walk away.
You asked for a cig-a-rette, I could-n't stop star-ing at your eyes.

This is going to sound a lit-tle im-pul-sive, this is going to sound a lit-tle in-sane.
Ev-er since when I first saw you, look-ing bored in that plas-tic chair.

Acous. Gtr. & Elec. Gtr. 1

I know you don't know me yet but you and I, we will be to-geth-er some-
With the lights of the of-fice a-round you, those blond streaks, they look so pret-ty in

1.
-day, some-day. I know, I

know I sound like I'm on drugs, but lis-ten to me now when I say...

Unemployed Boyfriend – 11 – 3
0467B

80

2.

your black hair. You look cool and al-ter-na-tive with that dis-af-fect-ed stare. You want peo-ple to think that you just don't care.

Chorus:

Hey, you can be with me, yeah, 'cause I just might be the one who will treat you like you're per-fect, who will al-ways make you come.

Unemployed Boyfriend – 11 – 4
0467B

G5 E5 D G5 E5 D
Cont. rhy. simile
Hey, you can be with me. Yes, I will al - ways let you
G5 E5 D C/G D/A
Acous. Gtr.
win. I will nev-er be like those oth-er guys. I will nev - er be your un - em-ployed
Verse 3:
G5 C(9) Em(9) C(9)
boy - friend. Can you be-lieve he said that to me? To me, of all peo-ple.
Elec. Gtr. 1
G5 C(9) Em(9) C(9) G/B G/A
Resume verse fig. simile
I can't e-ven re-mem-ber the last time a guy took me out on a date and ac - tu - 'ly paid for it.
fdbk.

w/Lead Fig. 1 (Elec. Gtr. 3) 3 times, simile
G5 C(9) Em(9) C(9) G/B G/A
This is going to sound a lit-tle bit out there. Yeah, this is gon-na sound a lit-tle in-sane.
Elec. Gtr. 3
harm.
G5 C(9) A7
Acous. Gtr.
I keep hav-ing the same dream, you will be the moth-er of my
Elec. Gtr. 1
mf
Cont. in slashes
Bridge:
A(2)
Acous. Gtr. & Elec. Gtr. 1
chil-dren some-day, (echo repeats) some-day! (echo repeats)
Cont. rhy. fig. simile
Vcl. dbld. 8vb
I heard you sleep with that ob-nox-

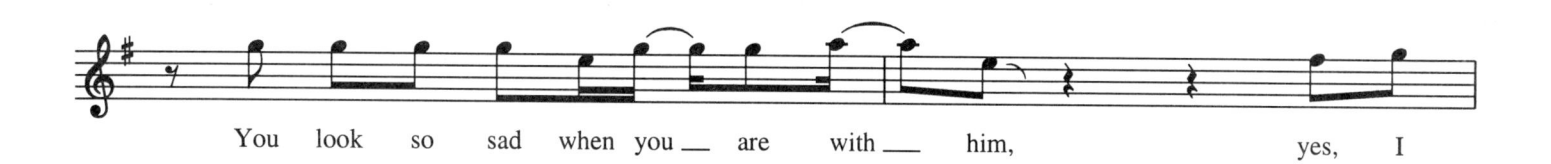

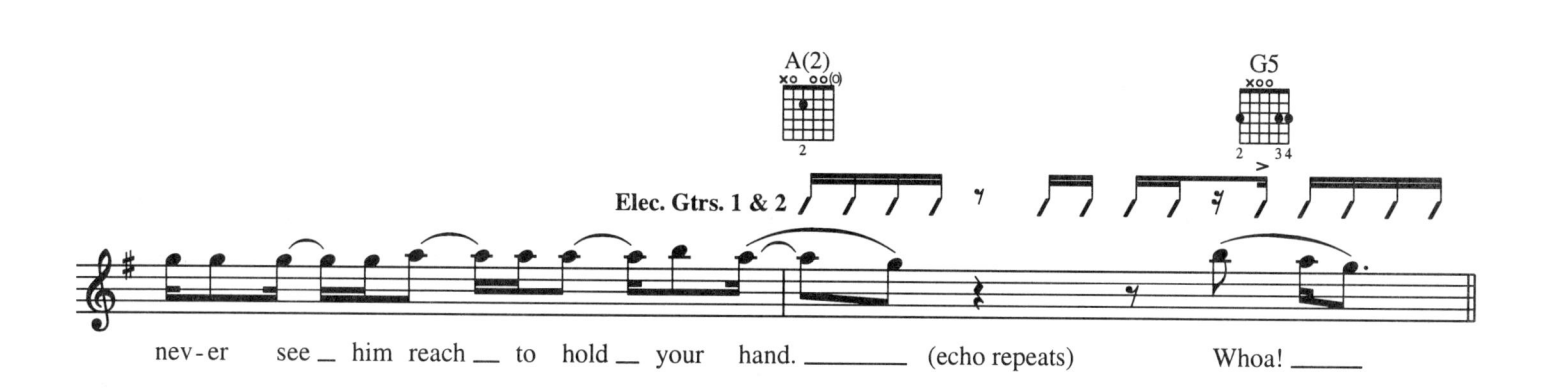

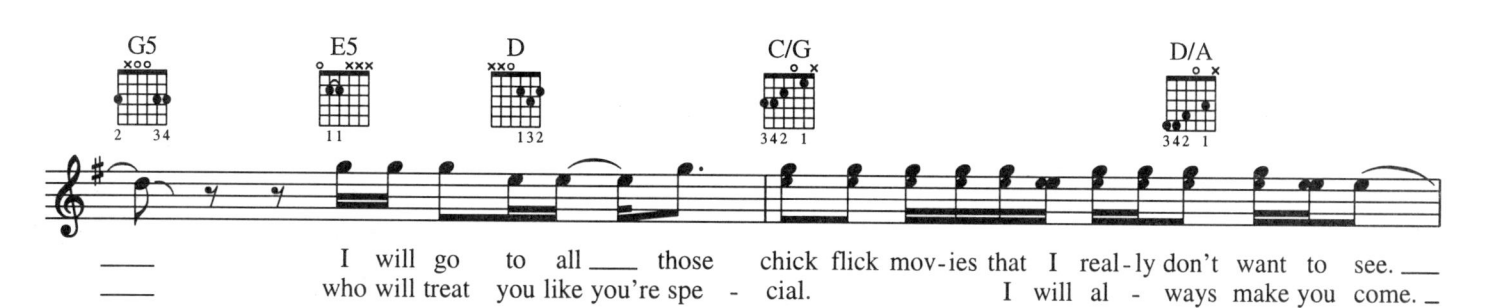

ious guy, I know he is in that famous band.

You look so sad when you are with him, yes, I

Elec. Gtrs. 1 & 2 — A(2) — G5

never see him reach to hold your hand. (echo repeats) Whoa!

Chorus:

E5 D G5 E5 D

Resume chorus fig. simile

Yeah, you can be with me. Yes, I will treat you like a queen.
Yes, you can be with me. Yeah, I just might be the one

G5 E5 D C/G D/A

I will go to all those chick flick mov-ies that I real-ly don't want to see.
who will treat you like you're spe - cial. I will al - ways make you come.

84

Yeah, you can be with me. No, I will nev-er let you down.
You can be with me. Yes, I will al-ways let you win.

I will nev-er make out with your girl-friends when I know you're not a-round.
I will nev-er be like those

oth-er guys, (echo repeats) I will nev-er be like those

oth-er guys! I will nev-er be your un-em-ployed

Outro:
Acous. Gtr. resume intro fig. simile

boy friend. (echo repeats) *Can you be-lieve this? I mean, can this be for real?* No!

*Elec. Gtrs. 1 & 2

w/fdbk.

*Composite arrangement.

Unemployed Boyfriend – 11 – 8
0467B

Then he takes my hand, writes down his num-ber and just walks a-way. Whoa!

fdbk.

Elec. Gtr. 3

harm.

w/Lead Fig. 1 *(Elec. Gtr. 3) 4 times, simile*

I mean wow! But you know the weird thing is he's ac-t'ly kind-a

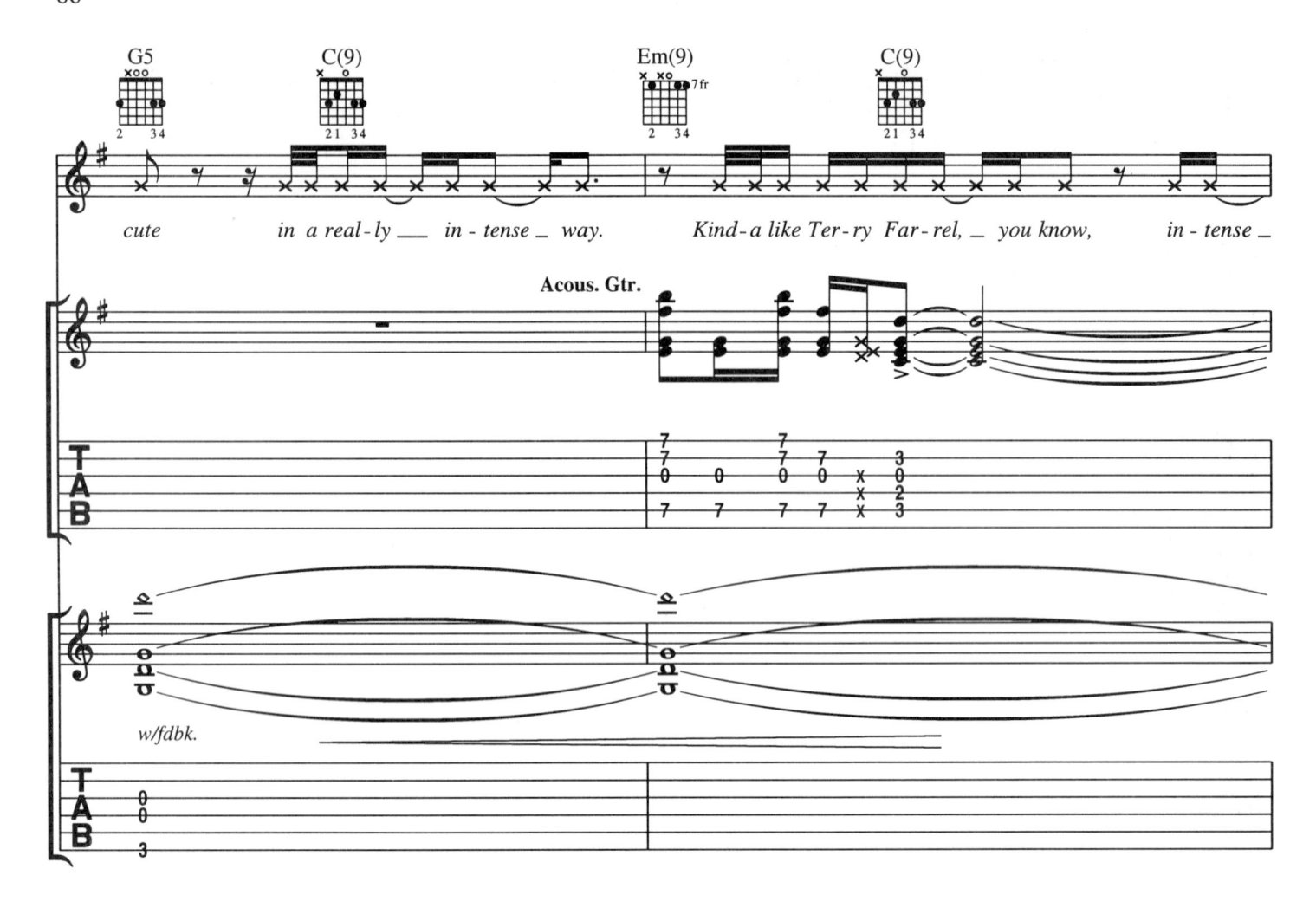

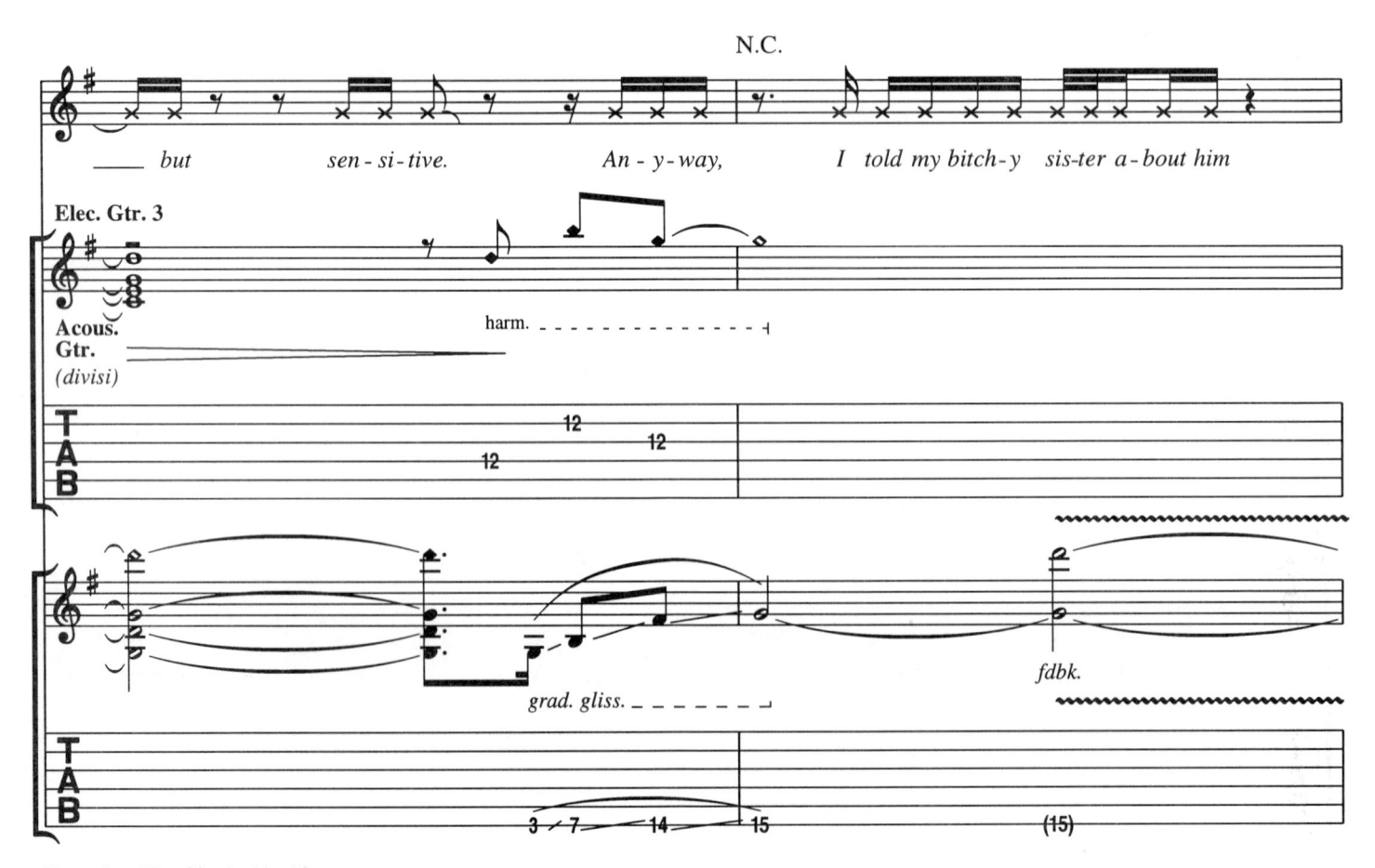

cute in a real-ly __ in-tense __ way. Kind-a like Ter-ry Far-rel, __ you know, in-tense __ but sen-si-tive. An-y-way, I told my bitch-y sis-ter a-bout him *and she just laughed at me. I told her I was real-ly ex-cit-ed a-bout this, that I have a real-ly good feel-ing a-bout this guy. I told her, this could be the guy. I'm like...*

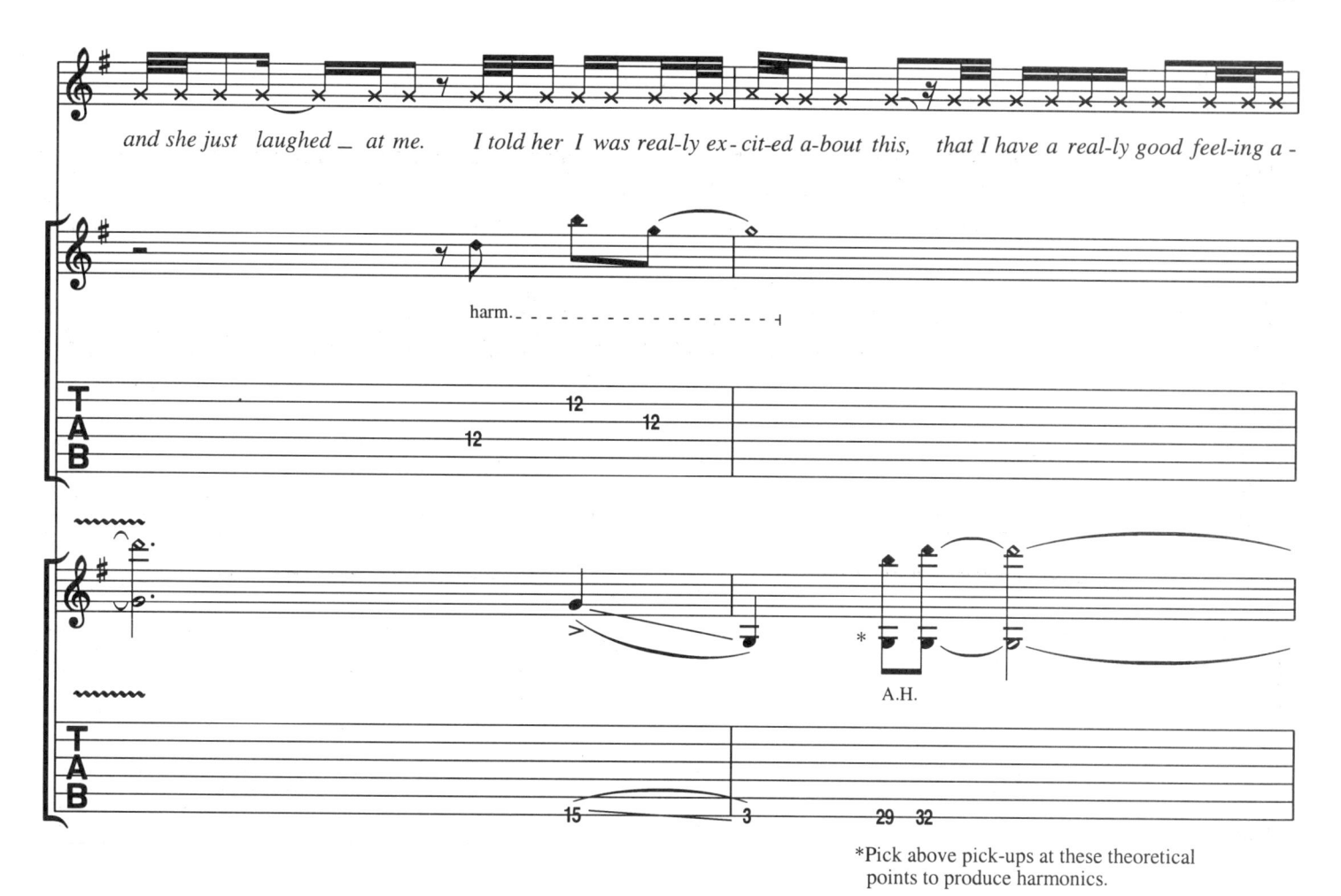

*Pick above pick-ups at these theoretical points to produce harmonics.

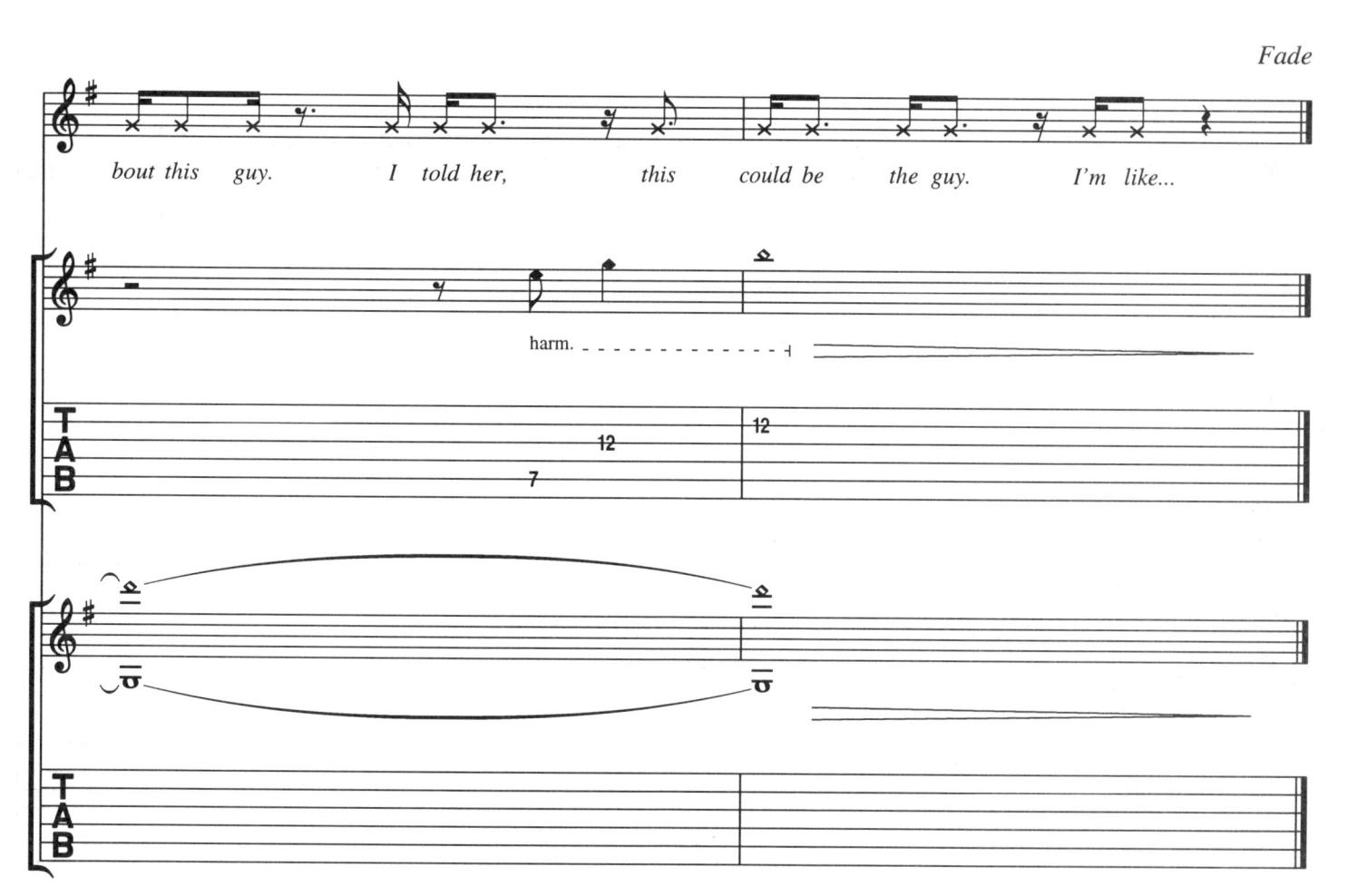

Fade

WONDERFUL

lyrics by alexakis
music by everclear

Moderately ♩ = 94

Intro:

13 sec.

Spoken: Hey, ain't life wonderful, wonderful...

Verse 1:
Acous. Gtr. 1 *(dbld. by Elec. Gtr. 1 w/clean-tone)*

I close my eyes when it gets too sad.

I think thoughts that I know are bad. I close my eyes and I count to ten. I

hope it's o-ver when I o-pen them. I want the things that I had be-fore, like a

Star Wars post-er on my bed-room door. I wish I could count to ten,

Wonderful – 11 – 1
0467B

© 2000 evergleam music / montalupis music / commongreen music / irving music, inc. (BMI)
all rights reserved

Verses 2 & 3:
D
G
(Em)
and make ev - 'ry-thing be won - der - ful___ a-gain. 2. I hope my mom and I hope my dad will
3. See additional lyrics
Elec. Gtr. 2 (w/clean-tone & fast vibrato)
mf
D
(Em)
C
(Em)
fig - ure out why they get so mad. I hear them scream... I hear them fight. They
D
G
(Em)
Cont. rhy. simile
say bad words that make me want to cry. I close my eyes when I go to bed ___ and I ____

D
(Em)
C
(Em)
dream of an - gels who make me smile. I feel bet - ter when I hear them say
Pre-chorus:
D
(Em)
C
*Acous. Gtr. 1
& Elec. Gtr. 1
ev - 'ry-thing will be won - der - ful some - day. Prom - is - es mean ev - 'ry - thing
hold throughout
*Composite arrangement.
D
G
when you're lit - tle and the world's / world is so big.

I just don't un-der-stand how ____ you can smile with all those

tears in your eyes ____ {and / when you} tell me ev-'ry-thing is won-der-ful ____ now. ____

Elec. Gtr. 2

Elec. Gtr. 3 *(w/dist. & chorus effect)*

Wonderful – 11 – 4
0467B

Chorus:
G
Em
D
Em
Acous. Gtr. 1
Bkgd. Vcl. Fig. 1
Na, na, na, na, na, na, na. No, na, na, na, na, na, na.
Elec. Gtrs. 1 & 2
Elec. Gtr. 3
Lead Fig. 1
end Lead Fig. 1
w/Lead Fig. 1 (Elec. Gtr. 3) 2 times, simile
C
Em
1.
D
Em
end Bkgd. Vcl. Fig. 1
Please don't tell me ev - 'ry - thing is won - der - ful now.
Na, na, na, na, na, na, na. Na, na, na, na, na, na, na.

Bridge:

| D | Em | C5 |

Acous. Gtr. 1 &
Elec. Gtr. 2

ev - 'ry - thing is won - der - ful now.___ I don't want to hear__ you say that
Na, na, na, na, na, na, na.

Elec. Gtr. 1

hold throughout

| D5 | G5 | E5 |

I will un - der - stand __ some - day. ___ No, no, ___
Bkgd. Vcl.: No, no,

| G5 | E5 | C5 |

Cont. rhy. simile

No, no. ___ I don't want to hear __ you say you
no, no.

both have grown in dif-f'rent ways. No, No, no, no, no. No, I don't want to meet your friend and I don't want to start o-ver a-gain. I just want my life to be the same,

E5
D5
C5
just like it used to be.
Somedays I hate ev-'ry-thing.
Cont. in slashes
T
A
B
D
All Gtrs.
I hate ev-'ry-thing,
ev-'ry-one and ev-'ry-thing.
Bkgd. Vcl.: Ev-'ry-thing,
ev-'ry-thing,
thing,
Chorus:
w/Rhy. Fig. 1 (Acous. Gtr. 1 & Elec. Gtrs. 1 & 2) 4 times, simile
w/Bkgd. Vcl. Fig. 1, 4 times, simile
G
Em
So please, don't tell me ev-'ry-thing is won-der-ful now.
thing.
Play 4 times
D
Em
C
Em
D
Em
Whoa, please don't tell me ev-'ry-thing is won-der-ful now.

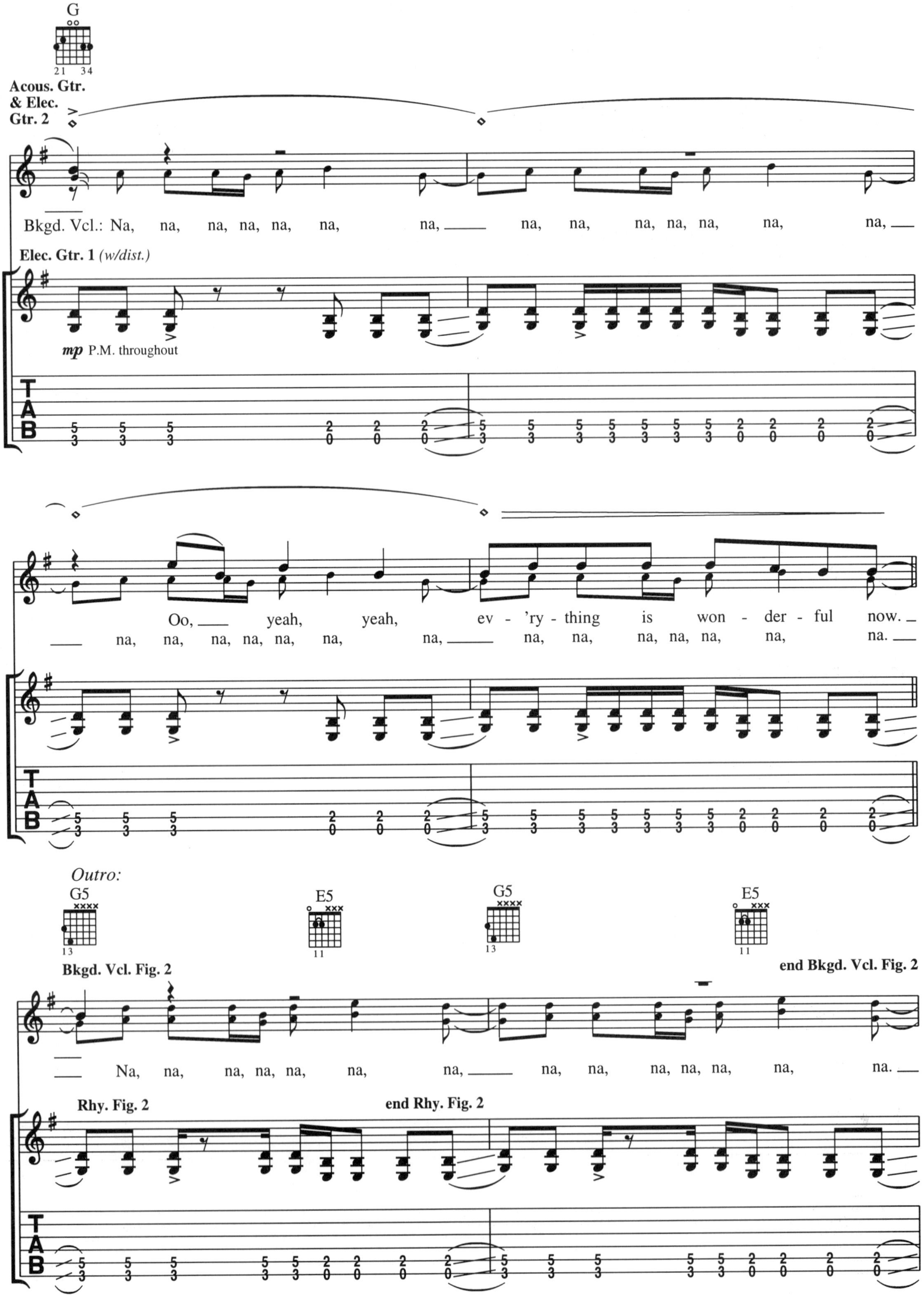
G
Acous. Gtr. & Elec. Gtr. 2
Bkgd. Vcl.: Na, na, na, na, na, na, na, ___ na, na, na, na, na, na, na, ___
Elec. Gtr. 1 (w/dist.)
mp P.M. throughout
Oo, ___ yeah, yeah, ev - 'ry - thing is won - der - ful now. ___
___ na, na, na, na, na, na, na, ___ na, na, na, na, na, na, na. ___
Outro:
G5
E5
G5
E5
Bkgd. Vcl. Fig. 2
end Bkgd. Vcl. Fig. 2
Na, na, na, na, na, na, na, ___ na, na, na, na, na, na, na. ___
Rhy. Fig. 2
end Rhy. Fig. 2

97

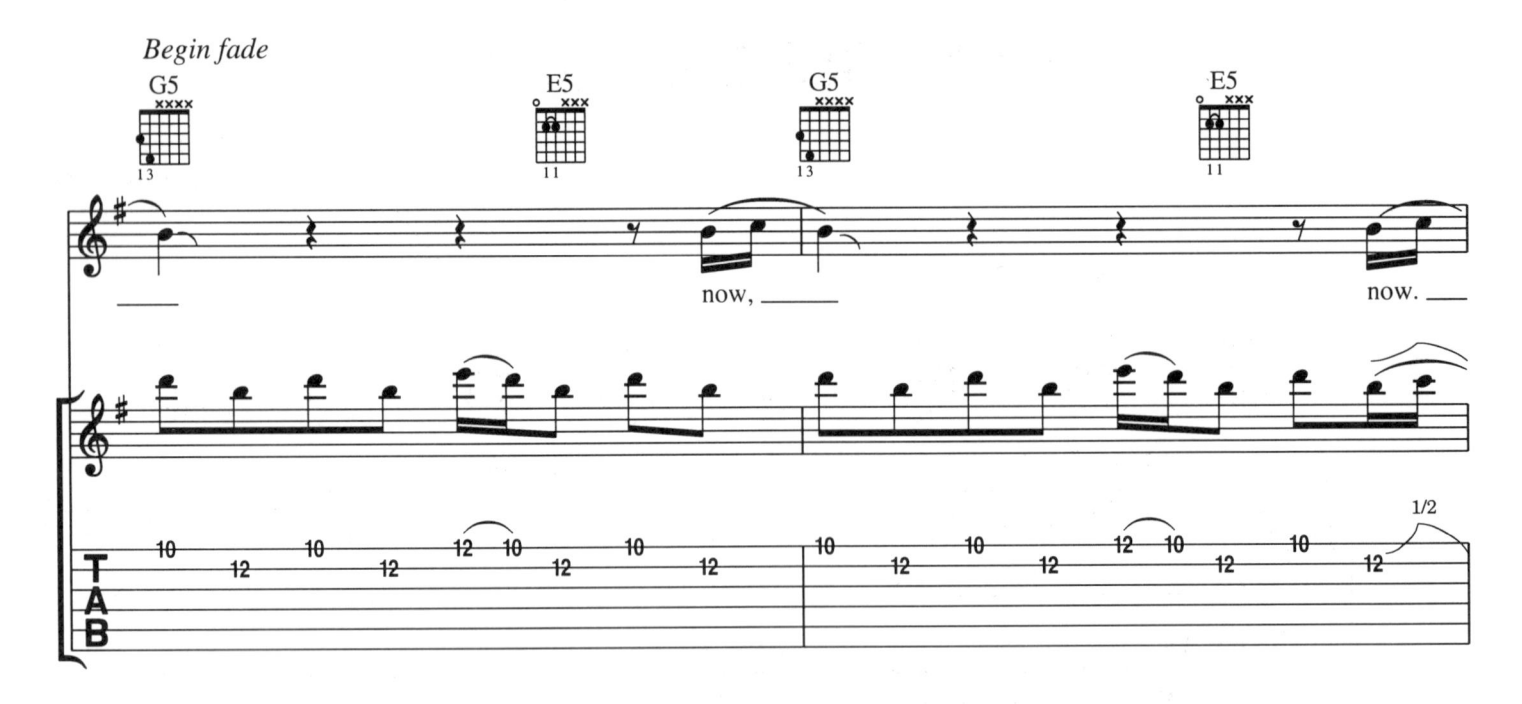

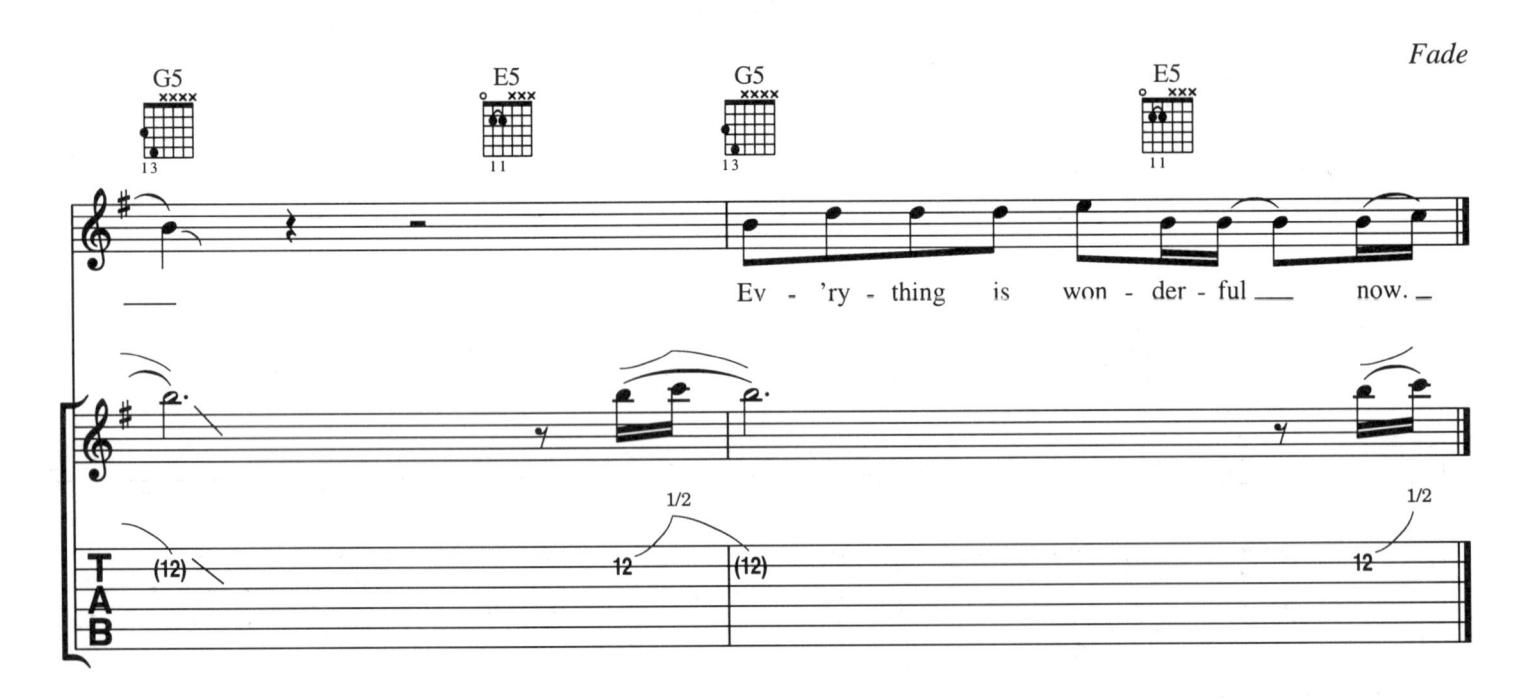

Verse 3:
I go to school
And I run and play.
I tell the kids
That it's all OK.
I laugh a lot
So my friends won't know
When the bell rings, I just don't want to go home.
I go to my room and
I close my eyes.
I make believe
That I have a new life.
I don't believe you when you say
Everything will be wonderful someday.
(To Pre-chorus:)

ANNABELLA'S SONG

lyrics by alexakis
music by everclear

Moderately slow ♩ = 86

Intro:

Bkgd. Vcl.: Oo, _____ oo, oo, _____ oo,

Acous. Gtr. 1
Rhy. Fig. 1 ... *end Rhy. Fig. 1*

mf w/thumb & fingers
hold throughout

oo.

Piano (arr. for gtr.)

mf

*Sounds 8va higher than written.

Annabella's Song – 7 – 1
0467B

© 1995 evergleam music / montalupis music / commongreen music / irving music, inc. (BMI)
all rights reserved

Annabella's Song – 7 – 2

Verse:

Em

1. Oh, I see you roll your eyes. You know it makes me
2. You know I'm nev-er home, I'm al-ways miles and a-way.

G6 **G5**

smile. You are like the sun to me, all bright as liq-uid fire.
I feel I'm run-ning out of time to say the things I need to say.

Em

I feel so pow-er-less to hold you up a-bove the world.
I call you on the tel-e-phone, you will not talk to me.

1.

You are quite a lot of __ trou - ble, __ for such a skin-ny lit - tle __ girl.

w/Rhy. Fig. 1 *(Acous. Gtr. 1) 2 times, simile*

Bdgd. Vcl.: Oo, oo, oo, oo. __
Such a skin-ny lit - tle girl.

2.   **Freely**

Yeah, you just don't un - der - stand, __ you are my ev - 'ry - thing.
Oo, __ oo.

*Composite orchestral voicing.

𝄋 *Chorus:*
a tempo
w/Rhy. Fig. 1 *(Acous. Gtr. 1) 4 times, simile*

An - na, An - na, tell me what __ you __ want, tell me what __ you need.
Oo, __ oo, __ oo, __ oo.

Annabella's Song – 7 – 4
0467B

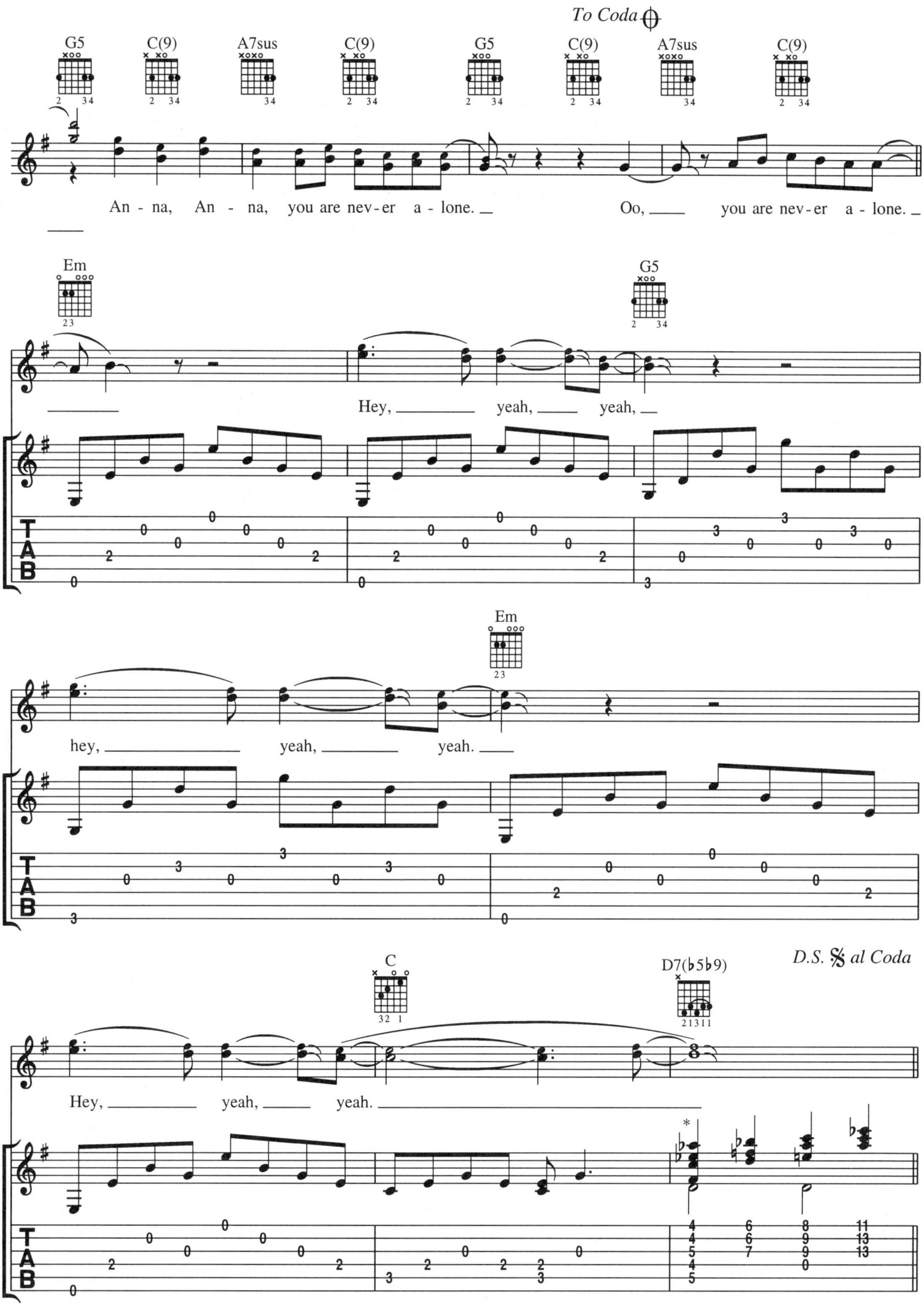

*Composite arrangement of orchestra/gtr.

you are nev-er a-lone. I like to watch you play when you don't know I'm there.

I see you in your sleep at night, reach out and touch your hair. I want to make this world

be just how you want it to be. Yeah, you just don't un-der-stand, you're my ev-'ry-thing.

*Composite arrangement of orchestra/gtr.

Chorus:
w/Rhy. Fig. 1 (Acous. Gtr. 1) 2 times, simile on repeat only

An - na, An - na, tell me what you want,

105

Annabella's Song – 7 – 7
0467B

GUITAR TAB GLOSSARY**

TABLATURE EXPLANATION

READING TABLATURE: Tablature illustrates the six strings of the guitar. Notes and chords are indicated by the placement of fret numbers on a given string(s).

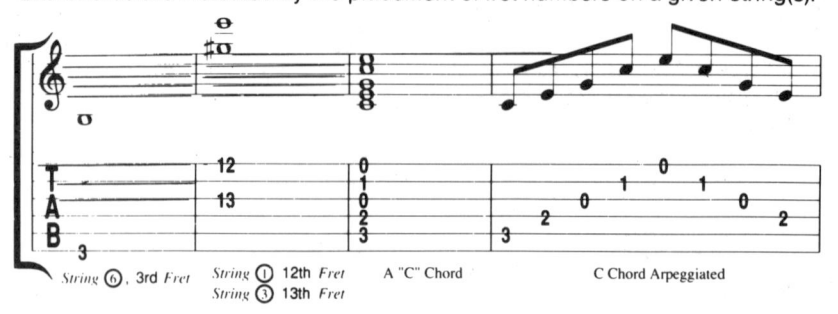

String ⑥, 3rd Fret   String ①, 12th Fret   A "C" Chord   C Chord Arpeggiated
                     String ③, 13th Fret

BENDING NOTES

HALF STEP: Play the note and bend string one half step.*

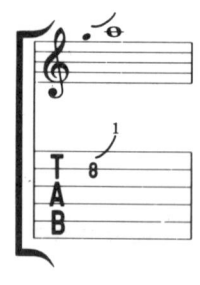

WHOLE STEP: Play the note and bend string one whole step.

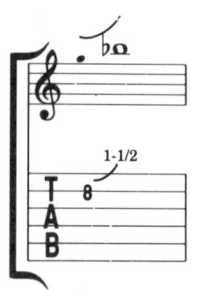

WHOLE STEP AND A HALF: Play the note and bend string a whole step and a half.

TWO STEPS: Play the note and bend string two whole steps.

SLIGHT BEND (Microtone): Play the note and bend string slightly to the equivalent of half a fret.

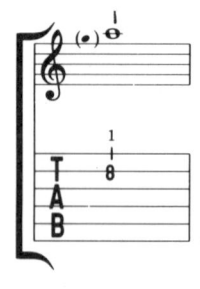

PREBEND (Ghost Bend): Bend to the specified note, before the string is picked.

PREBEND AND RELEASE: Bend the string, play it, then release to the original note.

REVERSE BEND: Play the already-bent string, then immediately drop it down to the fretted note.

BEND AND RELEASE: Play the note and gradually bend to the next pitch, then release to the original note. Only the first note is attacked.

BENDS INVOLVING MORE THAN ONE STRING: Play the note and bend string while playing an additional note (or notes) on another string(s). Upon release, relieve pressure from additional note(s), causing original note to sound alone.

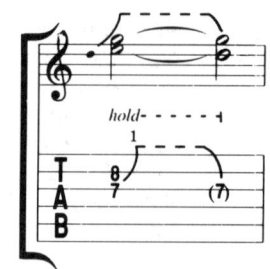

BENDS INVOLVING STATIONARY NOTES: Play notes and bend lower pitch, then hold until release begins (indicated at the point where line becomes solid).

UNISON BEND: Play both notes and immediately bend the lower note to the same pitch as the higher note.

DOUBLE NOTE BEND: Play both notes and immediately bend both strings simultaneously.

*A half step is the smallest interval in Western music; it is equal to one fret. A whole step equals two frets.

© 1990 Beam Me Up Music
c/o CPP/Belwin, Inc. Miami, Florida 33014
International Copyright Secured   Made in U.S.A.   All Rights Reserved

**By Kenn Chipkin and Aaron Stang

RHYTHM SLASHES

STRUM INDICATIONS: Strum with indicated rhythm. The chord voicings are found on the first page of the transcription underneath the song title.

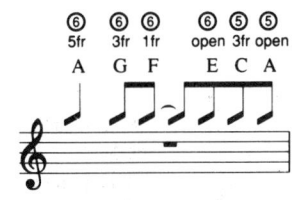

INDICATING SINGLE NOTES USING RHYTHM SLASHES: Very often single notes are incorporated into a rhythm part. The note name is indicated above the rhythm slash with a fret number and a string indication.

ARTICULATIONS

HAMMER ON: Play lower note, then "hammer on" to higher note with another finger. Only the first note is attacked.

LEFT HAND HAMMER: Hammer on the first note played on each string with the left hand.

PULL OFF: Play higher note, then "pull off" to lower note with another finger. Only the first note is attacked.

FRETBOARD TAPPING: "Tap" onto the note indicated by + with a finger of the pick hand, then pull off to the following note held by the fret hand.

TAP SLIDE: Same as fretboard tapping, but the tapped note is slid randomly up the fretboard, then pulled off to the following note.

BEND AND TAP TECHNIQUE: Play note and bend to specified interval. While holding bend, tap onto note indicated.

LEGATO SLIDE: Play note and slide to the following note. (Only first note is attacked).

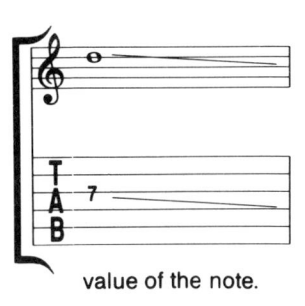

LONG GLISSANDO: Play note and slide in specified direction for the full value of the note.

SHORT GLISSANDO: Play note for its full value and slide in specified direction at the last possible moment.

PICK SLIDE: Slide the edge of the pick in specified direction across the length of the string(s).

MUTED STRINGS: A percussive sound is made by laying the fret hand across all six strings while pick hand strikes specified area (low, mid, high strings).

PALM MUTE: The note or notes are muted by the palm of the pick hand by lightly touching the string(s) near the bridge.

TREMOLO PICKING: The note or notes are picked as fast as possible.

TRILL: Hammer on and pull off consecutively and as fast as possible between the original note and the grace note.

ACCENT: Notes or chords are to be played with added emphasis.

STACCATO (Detached Notes): Notes or chords are to be played roughly half their actual value and with separation.

DOWN STROKES AND UPSTROKES: Notes or chords are to be played with either a downstroke (⊓) or upstroke (∨) of the pick.

VIBRATO: The pitch of a note is varied by a rapid shaking of the fret hand finger, wrist, and forearm.

HARMONICS

NATURAL HARMONIC: A finger of the fret hand lightly touches the note or notes indicated in the tab and is played by the pick hand.

ARTIFICIAL HARMONIC: The first tab number is fretted, then the pick hand produces the harmonic by using a finger to lightly touch the same string at the second tab number (in parenthesis) and is then picked by another finger.

ARTIFICIAL "PINCH" HARMONIC: A note is fretted as indicated by the tab, then the pick hand produces the harmonic by squeezing the pick firmly while using the tip of the index finger in the pick attack. If parenthesis are found around the fretted note, it does not sound. No parenthesis means both the fretted note and A.H. are heard simultaneously.

TREMOLO BAR

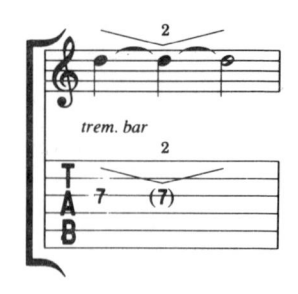

SPECIFIED INTERVAL: The pitch of a note or chord is lowered to a specified interval and then may or may not return to the original pitch. The activity of the tremolo bar is graphically represented by peaks and valleys.

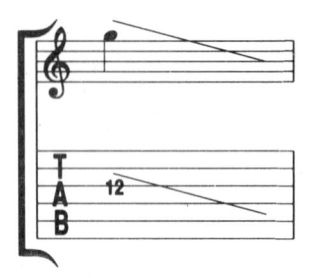

UN-SPECIFIED INTERVAL: The pitch of a note or a chord is lowered to an unspecified interval.